A CHRISTMAS MATCH: A REGENCY ROMANCE

LANDON HOUSE (BOOK 4)

ROSE PEARSON ·

LANDON HILL MEDIA

A CHRISTMAS MATCH: A REGENCY ROMANCE

Landon House

(Book 4)

By

Rose Pearson

A CHRISTMAS MATCH: A REGENCY ROMANCE

PROLOGUE

"Lady Charity?"

Lady Charity Forrest looked up from her book, seeing the maid standing in the doorway.

"Yes?"

"I beg your pardon, but your father has asked to see you."

A little surprised, Charity set aside her book and rose.

"Is something the matter?" she asked, but the maid only looked back at her blankly. Charity smiled to herself ruefully, realizing, of course, that the Duke of Landon would never say a word to a mere servant about what he intended to speak of to his daughter. That being said, it was rather unusual for her father to have called her in such a manner. The Duke of Landon, whilst always willing to do his best for his daughters, was not a gentleman who had any evident desire to be close to them. Charity enjoyed their conversations around the dinner table but, aside from that, nothing of any particular intimacy was ever discussed. "Where is he at present?"

"In his study, my Lady," the maid replied, stepping aside so that she might hold the door open for Charity to walk through. "He did say that it was to be at once."

All the more astonished, Charity made her way quickly towards the study, feeling a slight twist of unease settle itself into her heart. Surely there could be nothing wrong? They had enjoyed a very happy autumn, for her older sister, Lady Selina, had found happiness with the Earl of Barrington and had wed only a few weeks after the Season had ended. It had been joyous for Charity to see her sisters again, for there were now three wed and settled as mistresses of their own estates, whilst Charity, Maria and Dorothea remained at home. Her younger two sisters were, at present, engaged by their governess who had insisted that they practice their painting, whilst Charity, being a little older, was quite ready and prepared for her debut into society come the following summer Season.

Reaching the door of her father's study, Charity hesitated for a moment before she lifted her hand and rapped sharply upon it. Straightening her shoulders and hearing her father calling her to enter, she took a breath and stepped inside, placing a gentle smile on her face and hiding away the worry which had begun to take hold of her heart.

Thankfully, the Duke smiled at her the moment she stepped inside, and Charity instantly felt her heart lift just a little.

"My dear Charity," the Duke said, gesturing for her to move closer. "Come in, my dear. Please, do sit down."

"Thank you, Father," she replied, sitting down carefully so that she would not wrinkle her skirts. "Is something the matter?"

The Duke lifted his thick eyebrows, his green eyes twinkling.

"Nothing is wrong, my dear, if that is what concerns you. No, indeed, it is that I have had news from Lady Hayward and I thought it best to inform you at once about what has been decided."

Charity blinked rapidly, her anxiety dissipating.

"Lady Hayward?" she repeated, knowing precisely who the lady was, and wondering what this would mean for her. "I am to see her very soon, am I not?"

Lady Hayward had guided her elder sisters through society and, thus far, had done very well indeed in helping secure each of them an excellent match. She was aiding the Duke of Landon with his daughters in exchange for his guidance, support and aid with her own sons – the eldest of whom had taken on the title at a fairly young age. It was an arrangement which seemed to suit both Lady Hayward and the Duke and Charity had to confess that she was eagerly anticipating when it would be her turn.

"My dear, London is still very busy this time of year," the Duke replied, as Charity began to frown. "Some may call it the 'little Season', but I am of the opinion that it will do you very well indeed."

Her heart immediately sank low.

"You mean to say that I am not to wait for the spring Season, father?" she asked, knowing full well that winter in London was certainly nowhere near as exciting nor as fulfilling as the spring Season. Yes, there would be balls and the like, but there would not be as many of the *ton* present and, given the cold and the dark, certainly a good deal less for her to do during the day. There would be no sunlit walks through Hyde Park, no lingering conversations on the London streets. Rather, she would have to set her hopes on all of the other social events which would take place, few as they might be!

"You leave within the fortnight," the Duke said, with a broad smile settling across his face, making it seem as though she were to feel nothing but joy at this news. "Lady Hayward's son – the second of them – is also to be in London, I believe, in order to discuss a few matters of business with his solicitors and, if I am correct in stating this, in the hope of securing a bride!"

He chuckled, his eyes twinkling, but Charity could not find even a modicum of mirth in this remark. She had no intention of setting her cap at Lady Hayward's son, regardless of what her father might think!

"I see," she replied, with as gracious a smile as possible. There was no cause for her to complain, no matter if she did feel a little disappointed. To do so would be impolite and churlish, and she did not want her father to think that there was any ingratitude on her part. "Thank you, father. Is there anything that I need to do to prepare?"

The Duke shook his head.

"You will be able to purchase all that you require

once you are in London. Lady Hayward will guide your every step, as she has done with your sisters. I am sure it will go very well, my dear." Appearing now rather satisfied, he folded his hands and rested his arms on the table. "You will be glad to go to London, I am sure."

"Yes, father, of course." Charity forced a smile to her face and rose, realizing now that the conversation was at an end. "Thank you for making such an arrangement. I – I will be sorry, however, to spend Christmas away from you and my sisters."

A small smile lifted the Duke's lips.

"I am sure you will, my dear Charity, but it is something that you will have to become used to." His shoulder lifted in a half shrug. "After all, let us hope that, by next Christmas, you will be residing in your husband's home as mistress of his estate!"

Charity tried to keep her smile fixed in place, in the face of the sudden realization that this might very well be the last few days she had to reside in her father's house before a great deal would change for her. Much to her surprise, her heart began to quicken as though she were afraid and, whilst she managed to bob a curtsey and excuse herself from her father's study, the sensation did not leave her.

Pausing just outside the closed door of the study, Charity put one hand to her chest and tried to steady her breathing. Closing her eyes, she took in a deep breath and let it out slowly, telling herself that she was being foolish. She had been anticipating the Season, had she not? She had known that it would be her turn to go in search of a suitable match and had thought that she would be excited by it. Now, it seemed, she was actually a little afraid.

It has come sooner than you thought, that is all, she told herself, opening her eyes and dropping her hand. *There is just a little less time to prepare than you had expected.*

"Charity?" She looked up to see her younger sister Maria looking at her with wide eyes. "Are you quite all right?"

Charity nodded, managing to place a smile on her face.

"I am," she said, quickly. "Father has just informed me that I am to go to London with Lady Hayward – for the winter, not the spring Season."

Even though she tried to inject a little brightness into her voice, a little eagerness, she was not particularly surprised when Maria came a little closer and took her hand, looking up into her face with a true understanding etched there.

"It will be quite all right," Maria said, with such gentleness that Charity wanted to let the tears which had begun to burn in her eyes begin to fall. "That is something of a surprise, certainly, given that it is sooner than you expected, but you will do very well in London, I am sure."

The words seemed to stick in Charity's throat.

"I will miss you."

"And we will miss you also," came the quiet reply. "But it is your turn now, Charity. Your turn to be in London society, to dance, to converse and to enjoy all that it has to offer." She squeezed Charity's hand gently. "And you will find yourself a handsome husband and be very contented indeed."

Charity smiled back at her sister, a single tear trickling down her cheek.

"I must hope so, Maria. I certainly hope so."

CHAPTER ONE

"Now, let me look at you." Charity smiled rather self-consciously as Lady Hayward looked at her steadily, her eyes kind. "Your coloring is a little different to that of your elder sisters," Lady Hayward continued, after a moment. "With your auburn hair, you will need to wear colors which show it off to its greatest advantage." She tilted her head. "And your eyes..." A smile crossed her lips. "Hazel. I presume those were from your mother's side of the family, rather than your father's?"

"Indeed," Charity replied, a little surprised that Lady Hayward recalled such details. "I believe I resemble her a great deal."

Lady Hayward's smile was gentle.

"Then she must have been a very beautiful lady," she replied, as a faint blush warmed Charity's cheeks. After a moment, she gave herself a slight shake. "Your father has stated that we are to purchase anything you require – which, given that it is the winter Season here in London, may be a good many things!" She chuckled and Charity could not help but smile. "Certainly, you will need a few more gowns. And, in addition, a very warm pelisse and cloak, for I fear that we will step outside into the ice and frost many evenings over these next few weeks!" A small flickering frown creased her forehead. "And mayhap a new pair of half-boots?" Charity hesitated. She knew very well that her father had a great deal of wealth but did not want to be excessive when it came to her use of it. "My dear," Lady Hayward continued, smiling as she looked into Charity's face. "There is no need to concern yourself about purchasing such items. It is quite reasonable for you to have an entirely new wardrobe, and your father has been very specific that no expense is to be spared, just as nothing was held back for your sisters."

Letting out a breath she had not known she had been holding, Charity allowed herself a small nod.

"Then I would be pleased if we might purchase a new pair of half-boots also," she said, as Lady Haywood nodded. "And mayhap a new muff?"

"Two, in fact!" Lady Hayward declared. "And certainly three velvet hats, in differing shades."

Appearing quite satisfied, she turned to speak to the modiste, leaving Charity to look about the shop. Her measurements had been taken earlier, in the private rooms in the section of the shop reserved for that process, and now it as just a matter of finalizing the list of all that was required.

There was, in this establishment, to the point that Charity was a little overwhelmed by it all, practically everything a lady, or for that matter, a gentleman, might wish to purchase - for this modiste's was unusual, in that it shared premises with a tailor. Leaving Lady Hayward to discuss her specific requirements with the modiste, Charity continued to look at all that the shop had to offer her, trailing her fingers gently down a long silk ribbon which caught her attention.

"I do not know why you are so downhearted."

Charity could not help but glance up, seeing two gentlemen stepping into the shop, both stamping their feet to chase away some of the cold from their toes.

"It is not as though you are *required* to be in London."

The second gentleman grimaced, his eyes roving around the shop – and Charity looked away quickly, not wanting to catch his gaze and make it apparent that she had overheard his companion talking.

"It is better for me to be in company than be back at my estate alone," came the low voice of the second gentleman. "Although London is not a good deal better, I admit."

A little surprised at the irritation in the gentleman's voice, Charity turned away from the gentlemen entirely so that her back was to them. Thinking it best to make her way back to Lady Hayward, she began to slowly move back towards her chaperone, still permitting herself to study all that was there.

"There will be excellent company, I am sure," came the voice of the first gentleman, making no attempt to hide his words from Charity or Lady Hayward. "London may be quieter in the winter but that does not mean that there will be any fewer opportunities."

The hard, grating laugh which came from the second gentleman sent a flurry of surprise down Charity's spine and she started violently at the unexpected sound.

"You cannot call me your friend if you believe that I have any interest in seeking out such *opportunities*," came the reply, making Charity's face flush as she realized what he meant. "I have no intention of doing anything other than playing cards and being in excellent company at White's and the like."

"Then you are a fool," said the first gentleman, solemnly. "For you miss out on a the cheer and joy of the winter season, which might, should you let it, press hard against your melancholy and your low spirits, and refuse to allow them to linger within your soul any longer. And would that not be a good thing?"

Charity reached Lady Hayward just as the second gentleman finished speaking, putting a quick smile on her face as Lady Hayward glanced up at her. Part of her wanted desperately to turn around and look at the gentleman in question, to discover precisely who he was and why he was so set against all that London had to offer – in particular, good company – but propriety told her she could not.

"And when will those be ready?"

Charity listened as the modiste finished discussing the finer details of Charity's new gowns and various other items, before the modiste suggested that she have one final look around the shop and make certain that she had ordered all that she required.

"An excellent suggestion," Lady Hayward replied, with a broad smile. "Thank you for your assistance. We will do as you suggest." Turning, she caught Charity's arm for a moment. "The new cloak and boots will be with you in a few days' time," she told Charity, who was still doing her best not to look at the two gentlemen who were now just to her right, seemingly discussing something of importance. "And the muff and hats we will take home this very afternoon! And your gowns, of course, must be sewn to the first stage, before they are brought to the house for fitting. But I am certain that, within a sennight, you shall have all that you require."

"Thank you, Lady Hayward," Charity replied, feeling a small glow of contentment begin to fill her chest. "I look forward to receiving everything."

"And now, what about evening gloves?" Lady Hayward exclaimed, a sudden smile spreading across her face. "There is something that I did not consider! Do you require a new pair of evening gloves?"

Charity opened her mouth to state that she already had two very fine pairs – although none were new – only for them to suddenly come into the path of the two gentlemen. Given that there was not a great deal of space within the shop, Lady Hayward quickly excused them with a murmur, and made to take Charity elsewhere, only for the first gentleman to speak.

"Pray, do not allow our presence to prevent you from coming this way!" he exclaimed, as Lady Hayward stopped quickly and looked back at him, finally allowing Charity to do the same. "I was merely looking for a new pair of gloves for my wife."

He smiled at both of them, bowed, and then stepped back, gesturing for them to step forward. Lady Hayward hesitated for a moment or two, only for her eyes to light up and a small laugh to escape her.

"Good gracious, it cannot be you, Lord Ramsbury, surely?" she exclaimed, making the first gentleman's expression turn from geniality to confusion. "Already wed? And I thought that you would have many more Seasons in London before you would take a wife!"

Charity watched with interest as the gentleman frowned, then studied Lady Hayward for a few moments longer, only for his eyes to widen and his face to split with a broad smile. Evidently, he had recalled her and now stepped forward, reaching for Lady Hayward's hand so that he might bow over it.

"Lady Hayward!" he cried, sounding quite joyous. "My dear lady, how do you fare? It has been some years, has it not?"

Lady Hayward laughed.

"Indeed it has," she replied, smiling warmly up at him. "Last I saw you, you were..." She trailed off and the smile faded away. "You attended my late husband's funeral. I was very grateful to you for your presence, although I do not recall that I said so at the time."

Lord Ramsbury's smile softened but did not fade.

"Indeed you did," he told her, as Charity allowed herself to study his face, taking in the kind expression that seemed to warm his blue eyes, the small smile that spoke of understanding and kindness. "And how do you do at present? Are you quite well?"

His eyes strayed to Charity for a moment, just as Lady Hayward turned towards her also.

"I am very well," she answered, quickly. "Might I

present my charge for these next few weeks? This is Lady Charity, daughter to the Duke of Landon. She has only just been presented at court and now intends to spend time here in London." She smiled at Charity, who quickly dropped into as fine a curtsey as she could. "Lady Charity, this is the Earl of Ramsbury. My late husband and his late father were the very closest of friends, although I have not seen him since my husband passed away."

"And it has been too long," the Earl replied, with a generous bow. "I am very pleased to make your acquaintance, Lady Charity. You have just made your come out, then? Capital!" He smiled at her and Charity smiled back at him, struck by his sincere attitude. "Might I wish you every success this Season."

"You are very kind, Lord Ramsbury," she murmured, but he dismissed the compliment with a wave of his hand.

"I should also be glad to introduce my companion to you," he said quickly, "else I fear I shall be very tardy indeed with my good manners."

A sharp turn of his head and a small gesture had the second gentleman bowing rather hastily towards them both, although Charity noticed that there was no genuine smile of greeting up on the fellow's face. Rather, he appeared quite stoic, as though such an introduction brought him no pleasure at all.

"Lady Charity, Lady Hayward, might I introduce the Marquess of Hosmer?"

A Marquess, Charity thought with interest, as she curtsied towards him. *Although a rather irritated*

Marquess, it appears! She smiled to herself as she rose from her curtsey, taking in the gentleman's dark brown eyes and thin mouth. He did not smile and his furrowed brows and square jaw gave him something of a morose appearance.

"Good afternoon to you both," he said, his voice flat and without intonation.

Charity waited for him to say more, to ask her something of interest or to make some sort of remark to Lady Hayward, but the gentleman said nothing. Instead, he simply stood there, his conversation now evidently at an end.

Charity hid a smile, not feeling at all insulted or upset by his demeanor. After all, had she not heard him speak with evident irritation about being present in London? Why then would he now show any sort of delight at being introduced to new acquaintances?

"I – I should also be glad to introduce you to my wife, Lady Hayward, when there is opportunity," Lord Ramsbury continued hastily, clearly eager to speak over Lord Hosmer's otherwise notable silence. "She is in London also, but did not join us this afternoon, given the weather." He glanced outside and then grimaced. "Perhaps she was wise to do so."

"Mayhap she was, given that it now appears to be raining heavily," Lady Hayward replied, with a chuckle. "But yes, I am sure that I speak for both myself and Lady Charity when I say that we would be very glad to meet your wife, Lord Ramsbury." She laughed, her eyes twinkling. "I should take great joy in telling her all that I recall of you over the years."

This made Lord Ramsbury laugh in return and, for a few minutes, he and Lady Hayward spoke of years gone by, of her memories of both himself and his late father. Whilst Charity listened, she could not help but study Lord Hosmer, finding him most intriguing, despite the fact that she knew he had no interest in furthering any sort of acquaintance with her. He was, she considered, a little taller than Lord Ramsbury although certainly not by a great deal.

There was a broadness to his stature that gave him an almost intimidating appearance, and coupled with his dark, brooding expression, certainly would not make anyone eager to greet him! Charity tilted her head just a little, quietly wondering what it was that made Lord Hosmer so very melancholy and why he showed such little interest in being in London, despite having come to town instead of remaining at his estate. Of course, she could not ask him outright why such a thing was so, given that she would never reveal what she had overheard, but still, the questions continued to flicker through her mind and make her wonder precisely what it was that gave him such a dark appearance.

"Wonderful!"

Lord Ramsbury's loud exclamation caught her by surprise and she looked back at him, only to see him beaming at Lady Hayward.

"Then you are to expect an invitation very soon," he finished, bowing low. "And I will not keep you any longer. I have my purchase ready and shall quickly take my leave. Good afternoon, Lady Charity, Lady Hayward. It has been quite wonderful to see you again."

Charity bobbed a quick curtsey and murmured her farewell, noting to herself that Lord Hosmer did no such thing. Instead, he turned on his heel and made his way back towards the front of the shop without so much as a word, although Lady Hayward did not appear to notice.

"Well, that is fortuitous!" Lady Hayward exclaimed, as Charity glanced at her, dragging her attention away from Lord Hosmer. "Lord Ramsbury is to invite us both to dine, where you shall meet his wife! Indeed, I was also glad to hear that his mother resides with them both at present and I will be very glad to see her again." A wistful look crossed her expression for a moment, her eyes focusing on something across the room rather than on Charity herself. And then, Lady Hayward caught herself and continued to speak to Charity in a most practical manner. "That will be an excellent connection to have, Lady Charity, for they will be able to aid you in your introduction to society."

"That is very kind of him," Charity replied, as Lady Hayward nodded but turned her attention to the gloves.

"He is a very kind gentleman, from what I recall," she answered, picking up a silk pair and handing them to Charity to inspect. "I am sure his wife will be just as he is." Smiling at Charity, Lady Hayward let out a very satisfied breath. "Just so long as he does not invite that companion of his... Lord Hosmer, was it?" Waiting until Charity nodded, Lady Hayward clicked her tongue with displeasure. "A very rude gentleman, I must admit. Most improper to simply murmur a greeting and say nothing more!"

Charity shrugged.

"I thought perhaps he was merely glad to allow Lord Ramsbury to have conversation with you, Lady Hayward," she remarked, a little untruthfully. "Perhaps I was wrong."

Lady Hayward glanced up at her, then chuckled.

"You do well to consider others in such a good light, Lady Charity," she answered, "but in this case, I believe Lord Hosmer to be nothing other than a rather rude gentleman who shows very little interest in anything other than his own desires. But that matters not, given that I do not think we will see him very often here in London. It may be the little Season, but that does not mean you will lack for good company!"

Charity smiled and nodded, choosing to thrust all thought of Lord Hosmer from her mind. She did not need to know why he disliked London so, why he had remained so dull in his expression and his manner. Lady Hayward was quite correct to state that there was no requirement for such things.

"Now, shall we purchase these gloves and then return to the carriage?" Lady Hayward asked, sending a slightly concerned glance towards the window as she took in the rain that now made its way down the panes. "I think a warm fire and a tea tray will do us very well this afternoon!"

"I should like that very much indeed," Charity replied, honestly. "Thank you, Lady Hayward. I have enjoyed this afternoon."

"Good." Her companion smiled at her, her eyes bright. "For there is a good deal more to come."

"You cannot wear such a dark expression all evening, Hosmer." Benedict glowered at his friend but Lord Ramsbury took no notice. "We are to dine with company this evening and you will need to show a little more gladness at their company than the expression you *currently* wear," he continued, with a roll of his eyes. "My dear, you must encourage him!"

This was directed to the slender young lady who sat quietly in a chair near to the crackling fire, although when Benedict glanced at her, he could not help but see the glimmer of mischief in her eyes. He grimaced and picked up his brandy glass. Lord and Lady Ramsbury were very contented together and that, he had to admit, irritated him immensely.

"I think we should do nothing of the sort," came Lady Ramsbury's reply, as Benedict looked towards her again in surprise. "To tell Lord Hosmer what he must or must not do will only have precisely the opposite effect to the one you desire." Her eyes twinkled as she looked back at her husband, before finally looking towards Benedict himself. "Is that not so, Lord Hosmer?"

"I think that you have made me out very well indeed, Lady Ramsbury," Benedict replied, swirling the brandy around in his glass. "Now if only your husband might agree with you!"

He shot a hard look towards Lord Ramsbury but his friend's frown only deepened.

"Lady Hayward was very closely acquainted with my family," Lord Ramsbury stated, as though he had not told Benedict such a thing already. "My mother, in particular, will be very glad to see her again... although she is yet to join us."

A small frown flickered across his brow and Benedict could not help but smile. It seemed that Lord Ramsbury was a little anxious this evening, as though he wanted all to go well, but was uncertain that it would do so. Of course, Benedict knew that his current demeanor did not help the situation at all, but he did not want his friend to even *consider* the idea that he might be interested in courting Lady Charity. Indeed, he wanted to make it quite clear that he had no interest in any such thing and, in behaving in this particular manner, he was certain that he was doing so.

Part of him had been a little suspicious that the only reason such a dinner had been arranged was so that Lady Charity and he might spend a little more time in conversation and, of course, this had made him consider whether or not he would even attend – but the thought of sitting in his townhouse alone for yet another night, drinking his whisky and staring blankly into the fire, was not something that Benedict wished to do. Thus, he had agreed to attend, but had no intention whatsoever of making any particular conversation with Lady Charity.

"I am sure that your mother will be present very soon, Ramsbury," Lady Ramsbury said, gently. "Come now, you worry too much, my dear." She rose from her chair and went towards her husband, one hand reaching out to settle on his arm. "I know that you are concerned for your mother's wellbeing, but I believe she is quite contented here in London. It was good of you to invite her."

Smiling up at Lord Ramsbury, she waited until he let out a long breath, smiled and touched her cheek.

Benedict looked away. He had no desire to see any sort of fondness, nor even a modicum of affection between husband and wife. That brought too much pain into his own heart, too strong a reminder of all that had been lost to him. He had been the fool once, and would not permit himself to be so again.

"My Lord?"

Ramsbury turned quickly to see the butler standing framed in the doorway, his head lowering for a moment as he bowed.

"My Lord, your guests have just arrived," he stated, as Ramsbury nodded eagerly. "I will have them shown in at once."

"As quickly as you can," came the response. "I am sure they will be very chilled indeed!"

Over the last two days, the steady rain had turned to hail and sleet, making it feel a good deal colder than before. Benedict, who was well able to afford to keep the entirety of his townhouse warm if he wished, had ordered fires only in the study and his bedchamber, having had no intention of going anywhere other than those two rooms, given that he could take his meals in the study. Lord Ramsbury, however, had been a little more generous and had made sure that the library, the drawing room and the dining room were all warmed by a great fire, although the hallways would still remain cold, of course. Benedict grimaced. Should anyone come to call upon him – as unlikely as it was – he would have to greet them in his study rather than take them to his drawing room. A small, wry smile pulled at one corner of his lips. It was just as well, then, that he had no intention of having anyone come to call upon him.

The door opened and Benedict rose expectantly, only for the Dowager to step inside. Her eyes roved across the room quickly, before she spread her hands and smiled apologetically.

"I simply could not be satisfied with the maid's attention to my hair," she said, by way of explanation for her tardiness. "But I am here now. Your guests have not arrived yet, Ramsbury?"

"They will be here in a moment, Mama," came the reply, although Benedict did not miss the look of relief which ran across his friend's expression. "I am sure that Lady Hayward will be very glad to see you again."

The Dowager Countess of Ramsbury's expression lifted.

"I shall be very happy to be in Lady Hayward's company again also," she said quietly, just as the door opened again and their guests stepped through.

The butler quickly announced them and the two

ladies curtsied, just as everyone else in the room either bowed or curtsied also.

"Lady Hayward!"

Benedict watched with interest as the Dowager rushed forward, her hands outstretched as she reached to take Lady Hayward's hands in her own. It was clear that she was a little older than Lady Hayward but, despite that, there seemed to be a genuine friendship between them. Benedict picked up his brandy glass again, knowing that he was not needed to do anything more than observe at present, given that both ladies would need to be introduced to Lady Ramsbury, and Lady Charity would need to greet the Dowager also. Idly, he studied the young lady, taking in her gentle form and finding himself a little intrigued by the burnished bronze curls that poured around her shoulders from where they had been pulled back to sit at the back of her head. She was not at all unpleasant to look at, for her figure was fine, her smile genuine and there was a warmth in her hazel eyes that Benedict was certain could not be falsified.

Although you believed such things before, without question, he reminded himself, a darkness beginning to seep through his soul. *And look where such a belief, such a trust, took you.*

"And you know Lord Hosmer, of course."

The two ladies smiled at him and then were shown to their seats so that they might all sit together for a short while before the dinner bell sounded. Benedict cleared his throat, a little surprised when Lady Charity's gaze fixed itself directly to his.

"And you are only just come back to London?" the

Dowager asked, as Lady Hayward nodded. "But do you not have your own daughters to bring to London? I am sure that I recall you having at least one!"

Lady Hayward laughed.

"My daughter, Miss Sophia Clarke, will make her come out in a year's time or so," she said, as Lady Charity continued to hold Benedict's gaze steadily, clearly not in the least bit perturbed by the dark expression he had settled across his face. "At least, that is what I hope for. One can never be quite certain what will occur."

A harsh laugh left Benedict's mouth before he could prevent it. One after another, the other occupants in the room looked back at him in evident surprise, although there was nothing but a look of reproach on Lord Ramsbury's face. He was clearly aware of precisely why Benedict had allowed such a sound to escape him, whilst the others in the room all looked a little stunned.

"Forgive me," Benedict muttered, feeling a swirl of embarrassment settle itself in his heart, whilst heat began to climb up his neck. "It is only to say that I quite agree, Lady Hayward. One can never predict what will occur."

Lady Hayward's eyes flickered as she studied him, giving Benedict the uncomfortable impression that she was seeking to discover the truth behind such a remark but, as yet, could not find a way to do so. Benedict did not know what else to say, wondering if he ought to expand upon his explanation a little more, or remain silent, only for the dinner bell to sound. Relief poured into him as he rose from his chair, catching the slight smile on Lord Ramsbury's face as he offered his arm to his wife.

"Shall we make our way to the dining room?" Lord

Ramsbury asked, as they all fell into line. "I am sure that there is a feast awaiting us and I, for one, am certainly ready to enjoy it!"

His levity relieved the awkward tension which now surrounded the group, and allowed Benedict to breathe a little more easily. He had not meant to embarrass himself in such a way, and yet he had done so simply by his own foolishness. No doubt Lady Hayward and Lady Charity would think him a little odd, given that he had very little intention of making enthusiastic conversation with either of them. Not that he would be rude, of course, but certainly he would not be overly eager.

Walking into the dining room, Benedict stiffened just a little as he realized that he would be seated next to Lady Charity. His first instinct was that Lord Ramsbury had done so purposefully, only to realize that etiquette required it. Lady Charity smiled at him as she took her seat, forcing Benedict to return it with one of his own – which he managed to do without too much difficulty. Sitting rather stiffly, he waited until the first course commenced before allowing himself to relax just a little, praying that Lady Charity would not expect a great deal from him.

"And so you are to spend Christmas here, Lady Charity?"

Lady Charity nodded, looking up from her soup.

"I am, Lady Ramsbury," she answered, quietly. "It will be a little unusual for me to spend it away from my father and my other sisters but I am certain I shall enjoy it."

"And you, Lady Hayward?" Lord Ramsbury asked. "What of your own children?"

Lady Hayward smiled brightly.

"They are all to come to London for Christmas Day," she said, and Lady Charity seemed to brighten just a little. "We shall be a very jolly party indeed."

"Then I must insist that you all join us here for dinner," Lady Ramsbury said warmly, making Lady Charity catch her breath as she turned from Lady Ramsbury to look at Lady Hayward.

Benedict allowed himself a small, wry smile. Talk of Christmas brought him no joy, no eager expectation as there now appeared to be in both Lady Hayward's eyes and Lady Charity's expression. No, he would spend the day entirely alone, looking forward to when it came to a close and, mayhap, drinking a little too much liquor in the hope of forgetting.

"That is very kind of you indeed, Lady Ramsbury," Lady Hayward replied, sounding very pleased indeed. "I thank you."

"And what are your plans, Lord Hosmer?"

It took a moment for Benedict to realize that Lady Charity was addressing him. Setting his spoon down carefully, he glanced at her and saw the interest flickering in her hazel eyes.

"What do you mean, Lady Charity?" he asked, seeing the frown that immediately jumped into her features.

"I simply meant to ask what your intentions are for Christmas Day," came the reply, as a flush of heat crept into her cheeks and she glanced away from him, clearly a little embarrassed. "That is all that I meant."

"Oh, do not concern yourself with Lord Hosmer!" Lady Ramsbury exclaimed, before Benedict could reply. "My dear Lady Charity, one thing you must learn about Lord Hosmer is that this time of year is something that he deeply dislikes." One eyebrow arched as she looked hard at him, making Benedict flush as he realized that he had inadvertently embarrassed Lady Charity. He *had* known that she was asking him about Christmas but, given that he wanted to avoid the subject entirely, he had made a remark which was meant to brush her off and push her away from the subject. Now, it seemed, Lady Ramsbury chose to step in and, rather than preventing the subject from being discussed, was now about to explain all to the lady! "You will not find him at any gatherings or such things," Lady Ramsbury continued, with a wave of her hand. "There is nothing about this particular time that brings Lord Hosmer any joy. Therefore, Lady Charity, I would advise you to never discuss such a thing with him, but rather save your happiness and delight with all that you find in London to share with someone who will appreciate such things." Her eyes narrowed just a little as she held Benedict's gaze for a long moment. "Is that not so, Lord Hosmer?"

Benedict spread his hands.

"It is as you say, Lady Ramsbury," he admitted, without feeling any cause to pretend otherwise. Daring a look at Lady Charity, he saw her glancing up at him before turning her head away again.

"I see," Lady Charity murmured, her cheeks still flushed but, much to his surprise, seeming to decide not to ask any further questions. "Forgive me, Lord Hosmer. I was unaware of your feelings on the matter."

As he cleared his throat a little gruffly, Benedict saw Lady Ramsbury shake her head and sigh, clearly frustrated with him, but choosing, wisely enough, not to say anything. The conversation continued on from there, with the Dowager beginning to mention the many things she loved about the Christmas season, which made Benedict grow a little irritated – although a good deal of that sensation was, he realized, directed towards himself. He had not spoken well, had not made a particularly good impression on Lady Charity and had embarrassed her somewhat by his response.

Glancing at the young lady in question, he took in her rosy cheeks and the way she steadfastly kept her head turned away from him, and felt a prickle of shame creep down his spine. In addition, there was also a small degree of admiration for Lady Charity, given that she had not asked him anything further about his dislike of Christmas nor shown any indication that she had any interest in discovering it either. That was not at all what he had expected. There had been a few occasions last Christmas time when he had been introduced to various new acquaintances and, without fail, having discovered Benedict's sharp dislike of all that the winter brought, they had questioned him excessively about why it was so. Benedict had not told them, of course - there had been no reason to do so, for it was not something he shared publicly with anyone. Only Lord Ramsbury knew the truth and Benedict did not think that his friend had even shared the full detail of that information with his wife either. That was why he appreciated Ramsbury's friendship, for the gentleman was both discreet and entirely trustworthy. Not many men could say such things about their friends.

"Truly, Lord Hosmer, I did not mean to embarrass you."

Realizing that the quiet voice he heard speaking his name was none other than Lady Charity's, Benedict looked towards her and tried to smile, but it felt forced and awkward.

"You did not embarrass me in any way, Lady Charity," he replied, truthfully. "It was my own foolishness which made it so. I spoke a little out of turn and must now beg your forgiveness."

Lady Charity's eyes searched his for a moment, and Benedict quickly began to wonder whether or not he had made a mistake in believing that she was not interested in his reasons for disliking the Christmas season.

But then she gave him a quick smile, murmured that there was nothing he needed to ask forgiveness for, and turned back to her meal, making sure to re-join the conversation with the others, and leaving Benedict to his own thoughts. For the second time, Benedict felt his consideration of Lady Charity's character begin to improve, for it seemed that he had been right in his judgement of her. She was not about to ask him questions, about to demand to know the truth as to why he did not want to join in with all the delights that Christmas could bring. Instead, it seemed that she was to remain entirely silent. Was she disinterested? Or merely eager to make the very best impression she could upon them all by showing no interest in the matter?

Why should you give such a thing any consideration?

Giving himself a slight shake, Benedict picked up his spoon and finished his soup without another word. There was nothing more he needed to consider about Lady Charity, for he had no intention of allowing himself to improve his acquaintance with her. Yes, he had made something of a foolish mistake, but there was no need for him to consider it over and over. Most likely, Lady Charity would soon be throwing herself into society, enjoying all that it had to offer, and would not even recall this evening, nor the discussion which had taken place. He would fade into the background and would not be remembered by her at all – and that was precisely what he wanted.

Wasn't it?

CHAPTER THREE

The conversation with Lord Hosmer, the discussion about Christmas and his clear lack of interest in it, was not something that left Charity's thoughts for some time. Even though she had found herself enjoying all that society had to offer – even though it was still rather cold – Charity could not help but continue to wonder about him. She had to admit that there had been a good deal of embarrassment brought about on her part, since Lord Hosmer had been so blunt in his reply when she had asked him about his intentions for Christmas Day, but she had certainly appreciated his apology when he had given it.

There had been something in his expression, however, which told her that he fully expected her to demand to know why he disliked Christmas so, a wariness which perhaps suggested that he had been spoken to about such things before. She had, of course, wanted to ask him about why he had such an apparent and strong dislike of the festivities and excitement which came with Christmas, but had chosen to remain quite silent. It had not been only because she had known it was not her place to ask about such things, but also because she had not wanted to do so when he had been so clearly unwilling to discuss it further. Thus, she had kept her questions to herself – although they had not stopped spinning around her head since then.

"You look quite lovely, Lady Charity!"

Charity smiled back at Lady Hayward, turning to glance at herself in the full-length mirror for one last time. It had been something of a surprise to see herself so changed the first time she had worn a winter ballgown, had her hair dressed by the lady's maid and had been permitted many additional embellishments which she had never really worn before. She appeared to herself to be a good deal older, even though she had not aged significantly. There was something of a maturity about her now, she supposed, which Charity had to admit she liked to see in herself. This evening, she felt much the same way, although going to what was only her second ball did bring with it a quite a lot of anxiety.

"And you will do very well," Lady Hayward continued, as though she had known precisely what Charity was thinking. "I am sure that you will find many gentlemen wishing to dance with you this evening again." One eyebrow lifted. "Lord Amundsen was very taken with you, if I recall. He danced with you twice, did he not?"

Charity nodded, aware of the flush of heat that crept into her cheeks.

"He did, yes," she stated, as Lady Hayward smiled. "And he has called upon me once already."

"Then I am sure that you will have at least *one* gentleman to dance with this evening, although I am quite certain you will find your dance card filled. There is nothing to worry about, my dear."

Charity let out her breath slowly, settling one hand against her stomach for a few moments so as to push aside the tension that had begun to swirl all through her.

"I must hope I do not make any mistakes!" she replied, as Lady Hayward waved a hand as though to dismiss the idea. "I was very afraid that I should do so at the last ball."

"But you did not," Lady Hayward replied, slipping her hand through Charity's arm. "Come now, let us make our way to the carriage and, within the hour, you will find yourself quite contented, I am sure."

LADY HAYWARD WAS QUITE CORRECT, Charity realized. It had been a little over an hour and she was already feeling a good deal better than before. There was no real nervousness present any longer and, given that she had found her dance card practically filled already, there was nothing for her to do but enjoy the evening.

"And I hear that you are acquainted with Lord and Lady Ramsbury, Lady Charity," said one of her new acquaintances. "They are both delightful company, are they not?"

"They are indeed," Charity replied, as Miss

Netherton smiled back at her. "Are you acquainted with them?"

Miss Netherton nodded.

"I am," she said, eagerly. "I was very dear friends with Lady Ramsbury's sister, who is now also wed." She glanced up towards her mother, who was still in conversation with Lady Hayward. "I am sure that both Lady Ramsbury and Lord Ramsbury were eagerly hoping that I might make a match with one Lord Hosmer, who is a friend of Lord Ramsbury, but I was quite determined that such a thing should not be!"

"I am acquainted with Lord Hosmer," Charity replied, instantly a little intrigued as to what Miss Netherton might know of him. "I met him recently and he also joined the party at Lord and Lady Ramsbury's dinner."

She saw something shift in Miss Netherton's expression but silenced the urge to question her about what she knew of Lord Hosmer's dislike of Christmas Day.

Miss Netherton laughed softly.

"Then I will not pretend that the thought of wedding Lord Hosmer was one that sent a swirl of delight through me, Lady Charity! He appeared to be most disagreeable and certainly showed no interest in my conversation."

"I confess that I felt much the same in his company, Miss Netherton," Charity replied, truthfully. "I am only relieved that there appears to be no interest from Lady Hayward to encourage me towards him!"

Miss Netherton giggled and Charity could not help but join in, hiding her mouth with her hand for a moment.

"I confess, I do not know why he comes to London when he appears to have so little interest in all that goes on," Miss Netherton said, after a few minutes. "He comes to balls and the like, but seeks only to play cards or to remain in conversation with his acquaintances! He never dances, never seeks out new introductions and shows no eagerness to become acquainted with any particular young lady, even though he is very eligible indeed!"

Charity lifted one shoulder in a half shrug.

"I should not care to be in his company, even if he wished it," she answered, honestly. "I found him rather disagreeable and his lack of enthusiasm for anything at all seemed to bring a weight to the conversation and the company."

"Indeed, it is well known that he dislikes the winter Season, although why he continues to attend instead of remaining at his estate, I cannot know," Miss Netherton said, with a shake of her head. "I cannot imagine being so miserable when there is so much excitement to be experienced here!"

Charity smiled back at the lady and spread her hands.

"Nor can I," she replied, "so let us, therefore, think no more of him and instead turn our attention to others who are a good deal happier than he!"

Miss Netherton nodded, tilting her head and looking at Charity with a sharp eye.

"I did hear that Lord Amundsen sought you out the moment you stepped into the ballroom, Lady Charity," she remarked, with a twinkle in her eye. "He is an excellent gentleman, I am sure."

Charity laughed and shook her head, refusing to admit that she felt any sort of interest in the gentleman. Lord Amundsen was handsome, amiable, and certainly had been eager to show her a good deal of attention during their very short acquaintance, but Charity was not about to permit herself to consider him with any serious intent.

"I do not know him particularly well, but have found him attentive thus far, yes," she admitted, as Miss Netherton smiled. "But I am not at all eager to rush into furthering my acquaintance with him. I am here to enjoy the Season and that is what I fully intend to do – and so long as there is better company than Lord Hosmer available, then I am certain to be able to do so!"

Miss Netherton opened her mouth to answer, only for her eyes to widen and her mouth to go a little slack. Recovering herself quickly, she glanced back at Charity, before her gaze returned to over Charity's shoulder.

"The very gentleman you spoke of is approaching you, Lady Charity," she murmured, as Charity felt tension begin to coil tightly within her. "Goodness, I did not know Lord Hosmer was even present this evening!"

"Nor did I," Charity murmured, not wanting to turn about and look over her shoulder for fear of garnering his attention. "I am sure that he will not be coming to speak to me directly, given what we know of him!"

Miss Netherton did not answer her and Charity felt her stomach tighten all the more, realizing that what she had just stated was, it seemed, the exact opposite of what was to occur.

"Good evening, Lady Hayward." Lord Hosmer's

voice reached Charity but she did not turn to look towards him, feeling a small spiraling anxiety settle over her heart. "And good evening to you also, Lady Hamilton."

"Good evening, Lord Hosmer," came the quick reply as, reluctantly, Charity forced herself to turn towards the gentleman, who was still looking towards Lady Hayward. "How pleasant to see you again."

Lord Hosmer did not respond to this but, glancing towards Charity and Miss Netherton, quickly greeted them also. Charity dropped into a curtsey and murmured a welcome, but did not seek to enter into further conversation, although she had to confess that she found it most interesting that he had come to speak to them at all.

"Lady Hayward, I wondered if I might beg a quiet word with you for a moment," Lord Hosmer asked, surprising Charity all the more as she looked into Lord Hosmer's face and saw what appeared to be a rather grave expression there, which she could not account for.

"Yes, of course, Lord Hosmer," Lady Hayward replied, quickly glancing towards Charity and gesturing for her to remain where she was. "Might you stay with Miss Netherton and Lady Hamilton, Charity? I will only be a few moments."

Charity nodded, not looking towards Lord Hosmer at all.

"But of course," she replied, as Miss Netherton looked back at her with wide eyes, whilst Lady Hamilton nodded her agreement. "I will be quite contented here."

Quite what Lord Hosmer wished to say to Lady Hayward, Charity could not imagine, but rather than attempting to guess, she simply continued her conversation with Miss Netherton as best she could. Miss Netherton, to her credit, did as best she could to discuss the weather they had endured of late and whether or not Charity hoped to attend the ball at the assembly rooms in a few days' time, but Charity knew all too well that they were both considering Lord Hosmer and Lady Hayward's discussion more than anything else.

"I believe it is time for our dance, Lady Charity."

Lord Amundsen came towards her, stepping between her and Miss Netherton in a rather forward manner. Indeed, he did not so much as greet Lady Hamilton nor her daughter but fixed his gaze to Charity's, a broad smile settling across his face.

"Is it our dance already?" Charity replied, a little surprised that it had come upon her so soon. "Gracious, this evening is simply flying past me."

A small frown chased some of the brightness from Lord Amundsen's face away.

"I do hope that you have not changed your mind, Lady Charity," he said, as Charity hastily shook her head, casting an apologetic glance towards Miss Netherton. "I should be deeply despondent if that were the case."

"Of course I have not," she replied, hastily, accepting his outstretched hand. "The cotillion, is it not?"

He beamed at her and led her towards the floor, forcing Charity to leave Lady Hamilton and Miss Netherton behind. Her thoughts still remained on Lord Hosmer and Lady Hayward, however, to the point that she was not greatly enjoying the dance with Lord Amundsen.

"Lady Charity, I do hope that you enjoyed my call upon you earlier," Lord Amundsen said, as they progressed through the dance. "And the flowers that I sent to you?"

Charity kept her attention focused on the steps of the dance as much as she could.

"I did, of course, Lord Amundsen, thank you," she said, carefully, fully aware that he appeared to be very eager indeed to impress himself upon her and yet, for whatever reason, she was finding herself less than inclined towards him. She ought to be flattered by his attentions, she knew, but there was something about his manner which did not encourage her at all. Perhaps it was that he appeared to be so very keen to further his acquaintance with her, when she had practically only just arrived in London! That did not make Charity think well of him, for surely he could not know anything about her character as yet, so why then should he show her such interest?

"I should like to call upon you again, Lady Charity," Lord Amundsen said, as they passed each other. "Or mayhap we might take a short drive through London? I know it is rather cold, but I promise you that I shall make my carriage as warm as it can be for you."

Charity glanced to her right and to her left, silently praying that those near to her would not have overheard Lord Amundsen's declaration of interest in her. Surely, he could not be implying a closed carriage? That would be well beyond the bounds of propriety!

"I – I should think it would be best to discuss such things with Lady Hayward first," she said, stepping back into place. "Although you are very kind, Lord Amundsen."

Praying that this would be enough to satisfy him, Charity soon found herself disappointed with his reaction, seeing the grimace that crossed Lord Amundsen's face. It was as though he had expected her to thank him at once, and to accept without question, as though his company were the most excellent of all gifts. And yet, Charity felt herself suddenly uneasy in his company, a little taken aback by the expression on his face at her response.

Thankfully, the dance came to an end and Charity curtsied quickly, grateful beyond words that she would be able to return to Lady Hayward.

"I *shall* speak to Lady Hayward," Lord Amundsen said, taking Charity's arm and settling it on his own as though she did not have the capacity to do so herself. "I am sure she will be very glad indeed to have me keep company with you."

Charity did not reply, hearing the arrogance spreading through Lord Amundsen's voice and finding herself almost repulsed by it. How glad she was to see Lady Hayward watching her, with Lord Hosmer beside her. Next to him stood Lady Hamilton and Miss Netherton, although they spoke quietly to each other and did not pay her any attention.

"Lady Hayward, your conversation is at an end," Charity said, relieved beyond measure to be back with her companion. "I do hope that you did not mind me stepping out with Lord Amundsen. It was on my dance card."

Lady Hayward smiled but it did not reach her eyes.

"But of course," she said, looking to Lord Amundsen who was smiling genially. "Good evening, Lord Amundsen."

"Good evening," he replied, sweeping into a bow. "I shall return for you, Lady Charity! The waltz awaits us!"

With another flourish, he stepped away from them all, leaving Charity to look after him, feeling herself a little confused. For Lord Amundsen to go from a dark expression to an overly delighted one in a matter of minutes appeared, to her, to be a falsehood which covered Lord Amundsen's true emotions – and that was something that displeased her greatly.

"You danced very well, Lady Charity!" Miss Netherton gushed, as Charity turned to glance back at Lady Hayward, before allowing her gaze to rest on Lord Hosmer. His expression was one of grim discontent, just as she had seen so often before, but this time, his gaze was trained on the retreating figure of Lord Amundsen.

"Thank you," Charity replied, putting a smile on her face and forcing her attention back to the lady. "Now, it is the country dance next and I believe you are engaged for it?"

Miss Netherton nodded, even as a gentleman appeared by her side.

She did not want to discuss Lord Amundsen's attentions to her, whilst they were dancing, with anyone at present, although she could tell from the sharp glint in Lady Hayward's eyes that she was not particularly pleased about something. As Miss Netherton made some further remarks about the rest of her dances, Charity turned to Lady Hayward, suddenly realizing that Lord Hosmer had moved away, without explanation.

"Lady Hayward?" she asked, as the lady looked back at her calmly. "Is there something the matter?"

Lady Hayward's eyes flared.

"What do you mean?"

Shame flushed Charity's face. Mayhap Lord Hosmer had not wanted to speak to Lady Hayward about something to do with her at all, but rather about some other matter.

"I thought Lord Hosmer wished to speak to you, and you were gone from here for some time," she said, by way of explanation and wishing she did not sound so foolish. "Forgive me. I ought not to pry."

At this, Lady Hayward put a gentle hand on Charity's arm.

"There is something of importance that I must discuss with you, certainly," she said, quietly. "I shall do so at once, for I fear that, otherwise, you will be unaware of the danger that Lord Amundsen presents."

A bolt of fear kicked into Charity's heart.

"Lord Hosmer came to speak to me about Lord Amundsen, for which I am very grateful indeed," Lady Hayward continued, gently. "He is evidently aware – as I have been – that the gentleman has shown you a great deal of interest this last sennight."

"And I confess I have found him rather forward with such attentions," Charity replied, truthfully. "Do you mean to say that he is not as he appears?"

Lady Hayward held her gaze and then nodded.

"Lord Amundsen, it seems, is eager only for the

dowry that you would bring to him, my dear," she said, gently. "The man is not wealthy and to pursue you in order to encourage matrimony, to gain that dowry is his only aim. It is not the first time that he has pursued a lady such as yourself, according to Lord Hosmer."

A little taken aback, it took Charity a few minutes to regain her composure.

"I see," she said, quietly. "Then I suppose I should be very grateful indeed to Lord Hosmer for his concern."

Lady Hayward nodded slowly.

"I do hope that such news does not trouble you, my dear," she said, carefully, but Charity quickly shook her head.

"I have no interest in Lord Amundsen, I assure you," she promised, as a look of relief crossed Lady Hayward's face. "Indeed, he asked– only a few minutes ago – if he might call upon me again or even take me for a drive in his carriage, and when I reminded him that such a thing must be discussed with you first, he did not seem particularly pleased. It was as if he thought that I should be eager to consider such a thing, as though he expects me to fall at his feet in happy delight and accept his attentions without hesitation!"

Lady Hayward nodded gravely, letting go of Charity's arm.

"If Lord Hosmer had not said something, then I believe that Lord and Lady Ramsbury would have spoken up also," she said, softly. "We have made an excellent connection there."

"Indeed," Charity agreed, quietly, her heart quickening just a little. "I confess I do not look forward to dancing with Lord Amundsen again."

"And it is the waltz also, is it not?" Lady Hayward asked, a little grimly. "Well, it is best to simply remain as quiet as possible and show no indication that you are glad of his company. In time, I am sure he will learn that you have no interest in him."

"I must hope so," Charity replied, shaking her head. "And I will make certain to thank Lord Hosmer for his willingness to speak to you about this matter."

Something flickered in Lady Hayward's eyes, although her expression remained entirely the same.

"I am sure he would be very grateful for that," she answered, softly. "Very grateful indeed."

CHAPTER FOUR

B enedict looked at his friend with one lifted eyebrow, refusing to be drawn on the matter.

"You will not say that you have any interest in Lady Charity, then?"

"I have none," Benedict replied, firmly. "It merely came to my notice that Lord Amundsen was seeking her out and, given that I am attempting to be nothing other than a gentleman, I thought it wise to inform Lady Hayward of the matter."

Lord Ramsbury looked back at him steadily for some minutes, before letting out a long sigh and shrugging his shoulders.

"I am merely asking, that is all," he said, as though there had been no other motive than sheer interest in asking such a thing. "Lady Charity *is* a very suitable young lady by all appearances, and I confess, I had thought that –"

"You know very well how I feel about such a suggestion," Benedict replied, sharply, his heart beginning to quicken as a faint trace of anger slammed into him. "I care *nothing* for the young ladies of the *ton*. I have no interest in acquainting myself with them, calling upon them, courting them and certainly not even a thought of engaging myself to one of them!" He threw his hands up in exasperation, as Lord Ramsbury held up both hands in a gesture of defense. "I thought you would have known better than to even think such a thing, Ramsbury."

Lord Ramsbury did not appear particularly perturbed by Benedict's outburst, however. Instead, he simply dropped his hands and looked steadily back at Benedict, his expression quite calm. There was no hint of anger in his eyes, no sharp words ready to come from his mouth. Instead, there was that gentle understanding that Benedict knew very well to be a great part of his friend's character.

"Do you intend to remain in solitude for the rest of your days, Hosmer?" he asked, as Benedict frowned hard. "It has been some three years now, has it not?"

Benedict's lip curled.

"Indeed," he grated, hating the fact that he was even being reminded of such a thing. "And my intentions remain entirely the same."

"Then no heir?" Ramsbury challenged. "No son to continue on the family line?"

There a sharp retort came to Benedict's lips but he held it back with an effort. He did not want to argue with his friend but the questions he was asking irritated Benedict a great deal. It was not because they, in themselves, were frustrating but rather that they forced him to consider things beyond his current pain.

"You have a younger brother, I know, but he has responsibilities of his own, does he not?" Ramsbury continued, quietly. "Or are you happy for he and his sons to take on the title of Marquess, should you pass away without a legitimate heir?"

Benedict shook his head.

"There is time for such things," he said, a little thickly. "A match can be made easily enough, without any need for the entwining of emotions or the like. In time, I will select a lady for my wife and expect the arrangement to be made without difficulty."

He spoke with as much detachment as he could, fully aware that, until he could let go of his pain and his anger, there could be no such thing yet open to him. He would not subject any future wife to his cold melancholy, even though he had no intention of having any emotional entanglements with the lady whatsoever.

"And why would you subject yourself to that?" Ramsbury asked, looking a little surprised. "There might very well be happiness for you with another, should you only pursue it. A happiness which would encompass your heart, even though, at present, you do not wish for such a thing."

"I dare not trust any lady," Benedict replied, slicing the air with his hand. "From what I can see, they are all just as each other. They hide their true emotions and considerations from everyone, making certain that the gentleman whom they pull into their grasp is confounded and confused by their attentions and smiles, even though there is naught but falseness there. There is no true consideration for any gentleman of their acquaintance. All they seek is a good title and a decent amount of wealth – and should someone appear who might offer them a little more than what they have at present before them, there is not even the smallest chance that they will consider anything other than their own position and wealth." With a slight curl of his lip, Benedict finished his diatribe. "When the time comes, I will find a lady who will be grateful to me for offering her my hand in marriage, who will not be able to find a better, more suitable match than I. That way, I will be quite certain that she will never turn away from me."

His speech now at an end, Benedict sat back in his chair, hearing the blood roar in his ears and feeling a strange sense of satisfaction that he had spoken so. It had felt rather pleasing to be able to speak as he had done, to explain to Ramsbury precisely how he felt. That way, he was sure, there would be no further questions as regarded Lady Charity, or any other young lady for that matter!

"I do believe, Hosmer," Ramsbury began, "that you have just greatly insulted my wife."

A cold wind seemed to sweep around Benedict as, startled, he looked at his friend to see a dark, heavy frown begin to sweep across Ramsbury's brow.

"I – I do not see how I have done so," he began to murmur, only for Ramsbury to hold up his hand, silencing him.

"You have just said that all ladies are just the same as each other," Ramsbury continued, his voice dropping low. "You have said that they seek only fortune and title and that they hide the truth of their emotions from the gentlemen who court them whilst presenting an eager and excited demeanor to us. Does that mean, then, that you believe that everything my wife has ever said to me, everything that was shared between us whilst we were courting, was nothing more than a falsehood?" Benedict began to stutter, realizing that he had made something of a misstep. "That she must not truly care for me, as she states, even though we are wed and have made such a confession to each other on multiple occasions," Ramsbury continued, his eyes a little narrowed as he looked back at Benedict. "That the words of love she speaks are naught but a pretense, said only so that she might please me in some way. Is that not so?"

"Come now, Ramsbury, you know that I did not mean to insult you," Benedict replied, his heart thumping rather painfully in his chest as the satisfaction he had only just begun to feel now began to slip away from him. "I certainly did not mean to include Lady Ramsbury in such a statement."

"But you said that *all* ladies are of the same ilk," Ramsbury stated, using Benedict's own words to fling confusion and misunderstanding back at him. "Either they are, or they are not. You cannot simply single out Lady Ramsbury as the exception." Benedict opened his mouth to argue that yes, he could do so, but Ramsbury had not finished. "You say that Lady Ramsbury is *not* the sort of lady you are describing, that she is the exception to your description of the ladies of the *ton*, but I believe that you say so simply because you know her and are aware that she speaks the truth when she tells me of the emotions in her heart. You cannot bring yourself to believe that there is any deception within her, cannot accept that, despite your claim, Lady Ramsbury could possibly be lying to me in order to keep me contented and happy. You believe that the words she states are all quite true because you *know* her and trust her. Is that not so?"

Lapsing into silence for fear that he might speak poorly again, Benedict gave his friend a jerky nod.

"Then why is it that you are so determined to believe that there could not be another exception or two?" Ramsbury asked, his tone now gentling as he shook his head. "Lady Ramsbury is not as you yourself have stated. She speaks honestly, loves openly and demands nothing from me. She will not turn away just because another might offer her something more, regardless of whether we are wed or not. Is it so truly difficult to believe that there might be another young lady with such qualities in London?"

It felt as though he had walked into a trap of his own making. Lowering his head, Benedict swept one hand over his eyes and let out a small groan.

"You do not like that I challenge you but I shall continue to do so," Ramsbury said, calmly. "It is not fair of you to speak in such a manner and to taint all of the young ladies of London in the same fashion. I am aware that you were greatly injured by Lady Frederica's actions but I do wish that you would not permit that injury to pull you away from any potential happiness that might simply be waiting for you, should you only be willing to seek it out."

Lifting his head, Benedict closed his eyes for a moment and then let out his breath slowly.

"I can see what you are saying, Ramsbury and I must apologize to you profusely for my foolish words," he admitted, feeling greatly uncomfortable that he had to now apologize and take back what he had just pronounced. "I did not mean to insult your dear wife. I know that there is a good deal of care and consideration between you both and –"

"She loves me ardently, Hosmer," Ramsbury interrupted, firmly, "and I love her also. There is such happiness and joy in my heart and in my home because of such a thing. I only wish that you would open your heart to finding such a thing also, instead of remaining so fixed in your pain."

Benedict frowned, wanting to argue that he was not wallowing in his suffering and that he was quite contented to simply wait until a time of his choosing to settle on a bride, but something in Ramsbury's voice told him that there would be no good in doing so. A slight stab of guilt entered his heart. Was it true that he simply could not let go – or was *choosing* not to let go – of his anger and pain? Was it something that he was deliberately choosing, so that he would not have to let himself consider what it was he wanted, what he sought?

So that you do not have to consider any young ladies of the ton?

"My dear Hosmer, we have been friends for a long time," Ramsbury said, finally pushing himself out of his chair and going to pour himself a whisky, then bringing one over to Benedict also. "I know that you did not mean to insult Lady Ramsbury but yet, in stating such things in a cold and calculated manner, you have done so. It is not something that will trouble me, however, for I quite understand why you have chosen to speak so and therefore, I will not hold a grudge or demand that you apologize."

"Thank you," Benedict muttered, taking the glass from his friend and seeing the small smile spreading across Ramsbury's face.

"However," Ramsbury continued, "I would ask that you think on what I have said, Hosmer. Consider that there might be another lady such as Lady Ramsbury out in London. One who might not be as eager to claim fortune and title as you suggest. One who might be open to finding a happiness with a gentleman of her own choosing, rather than being satisfied with an arrangement. One who might come to care for you as deeply as you once cared for Lady Frederica."

Benedict's lip curled as pain slammed into his chest.

"I care nothing for her now, of course," he stated, firmly. "And I feel that to allow myself to do such a thing again, to allow my heart to be so involved, would be nothing short of foolishness."

"That is where you are mistaken," Ramsbury replied, with a grin. "Quite mistaken. It may have been deeply hurtful and, I will not pretend that it did not bring you a great deal of sorrow and suffering, but to simply push aside the possibility of future happiness because of being so gravely injured is *not* wise."

Benedict shook his head but did not answer. He did not want to speak of Lady Frederica, the lady he had once believed himself to love with such a deep and ardent affection that it had taken over his entire being. He had never felt such pain as when he had discovered that, instead of accepting his offer of marriage, she intended to permit the Marquess of Norwich to court her. She, who had given him so much hope, who had practically given him her promise, had proven fickle and, with that had come a great deal of pain. Of course, in due course, Lady Frederica had wed the Marquess of Norwich, leaving Benedict to his own misery and grief and, since that moment, he had vowed never again to permit himself to trust a lady of the *ton*. Never again would he allow one of them to invade his heart, or allow himself to feel anything for a lady who drew near to him. They were all just as Lady Frederica had been, he told himself. There was nothing of truth in any of their words, in any of their looks or their declarations.

And yet, he had to admit that Lady Ramsbury was not so. And if he was to admit to that, then that meant that there might be other young ladies who were also as she was. That was a thought he did not want to consider at present, finding it much easier to wallow in his own grief and upset, to linger in his pain and to find himself settling there rather than seeking out a new path.

"I have confused you by my words, I can tell," Ramsbury said, his expression now back to one of joviality. "But that is a good thing, I think. Better for you to consider what has been said rather than believing that you are entirely in the right."

Benedict wanted to shake his head and state that he would much have preferred to have been permitted to remain in such a frame of mind rather than being challenged by Ramsbury but instead, he simply lifted his glass of whisky in a toast and then took a sip.

"And you *are* attending the ball this evening, are you not?" Ramsbury asked, before taking a sip of his own whisky. "The ball at the assembly rooms is usually a very fine one indeed."

"I have a ticket," Benedict replied, glad that they would no longer be discussing Lady Frederica or his own feelings towards the ladies of the *ton*. "I intend to join you there."

"Capital," Ramsbury grinned. "Who knows? You might even step out to dance this evening, and then what shock shall go around London!"

Grimacing, Benedict shook his head.

"I can assure you that I shall not do so," he stated, quite firmly. "I am not as easily changed as all that, Ramsbury, despite your best efforts." Seeing the smile fade just a little from his friend's face, Benedict let out a long sigh. "I am very glad for you, Ramsbury. I am happy that you have found such a beautiful contentment for both yourself and Lady Ramsbury. But that, I believe, is a very rare thing indeed and something that must be treasured, as I know you do. However, whilst I will confess that I have been persuaded to rethink my words and my belief that all ladies of the *ton* are just as Lady Frederica, that will not, at present, permit me to change my ways. I still dislike this time of year, regardless of whether or not I feel any differently about the ladies that surround me. It is best for me to be here in London so that I do not sink into a dark pit of despair, but that does not mean that I shall have anything to do with the *ton*. I shall not dance, shall not converse, shall not give any young lady even a hint that I am interested in her in any way." Taking another sip of his brandy, Benedict shook his head. "No, Ramsbury. I shall remain just as I am at present. Of that, I am quite determined."

CHAPTER FIVE

Charity could not help but feel a swirl of excitement run through her as she made her way into the assembly rooms. They had been done up very well, with green ivy snaking up the pillars near to her and holly berries entwined with fresh greenery that ran all along the sides of the room. The large fire and the many guests present meant that she could step out of her cloak rather quickly and, whilst there was still a slight chill in the room, Charity was quite certain it would not linger for long.

"A wonderful sight, is it not?" Lady Hayward said, happily. "I recall what it was like when I was present in London as a debutante. To see such decoration as this always made me very happy indeed."

"As it does now?" Charity asked, as Lady Hayward laughed and nodded. "I confess that I was a little disheartened that I should not be coming to London in the spring but, now that I am here, now that I have attended balls, soirees and the like, I have found it to be all quite wonderful." She smiled back at her chaperone, who had begun to nod in understanding. "It is not that I am ungrateful, you understand."

Lady Hayward shook her head. "I should never think you ungrateful," she said, firmly. "I quite understand that you were hoping for a spring Season but given that both your younger sisters will soon be out, I believe your father hoped to have you wed and settled very soon indeed." Her eyes twinkled. "But if there is no-one of interest in London at present, then I will be very glad indeed to return with you to London in the spring, my dear Lady Charity. I am certain that you will make an excellent match, although I would also hope that any gentlemen who approach you will be well considered and very well acquainted with you, before you would even think of accepting anything from them."

What had started as an easy conversation now grew into something a little more serious and Charity found herself nodding, wanting to reassure Lady Hayward that she understood precisely what she meant.

"I have had my sister Selina speak to me about such a thing," she said softly, as surprise jumped into Lady Hayward's eyes. "She stated that she had found such great happiness with Lord Barrington that she could never even imagine marrying a gentleman for nothing more than practicality." Seeing the gentle smile cross Lady Hayward's face, Charity let out a long breath and continued on. "She encouraged me to find a gentleman who was not just suitable in terms of his title and his fortune, but to seek out someone who might affect my heart also. Someone who is considerate, kind and generous. A gentleman who shows interest in my wellbeing rather than simply thinking that I will be an excellent adornment on his arm."

"Precisely," Lady Hayward agreed, happily. "I can only hope that you are willing to seek out such a gentleman, Lady Charity? It may take a little more time and certainly it can sometimes be difficult to ascertain whether or not a gentleman is being entirely honest in the character he presents, but I believe, truly believe, that it is worth the struggle."

"And that is why you would be glad to return with me to London in the spring Season?" Charity asked, as Lady Hayward nodded. "That is very good of you, Lady Hayward."

Her chaperone smiled back at her although, for a moment, Charity was sure that she saw a hint of sadness in the lady's eyes.

"My dear, I was blessed with such a gentleman myself," she told Charity, who quickly realized that Lady Hayward spoke of her late husband. "He cared for me deeply, as well as for the children. The love that he had for all of us was not something that I took for granted, for I knew that not every marriage was blessed with something so wonderful. And yet, those years were the happiest of my life, Charity. Now that I am without him, I feel such a great, lingering pain within my heart - but I shall never regret having such an openness and a love between us. It flooded my life with all manner of wonderful things and, therefore, that is what I would wish to see you find also. A gentleman who has a willingness and an openness to love you with his whole heart, rather than seeing you simply as the daughter of a Duke, whose dowry and inheritance will suit them very well indeed."

Charity scowled, her eyes sharp for a moment as she looked about the room.

"Indeed, I should not like that either," she stated, firmly. "Lord Amundsen was precisely such a gentleman and I confess that I thought very poorly of him."

"As did I," Lady Hayward replied, solemnly. "But that does not mean that all gentlemen are as he. There may be some who are eager to make your acquaintance simply because they have a genuine interest in you."

For a moment, a vision of Lord Hosmer flashed into Charity's mind but, quickly, she pushed it away. Lord Hosmer *had* been interested in her wellbeing, but not for the reasons she might have thought. He was simply doing so to be a gentleman, unwilling to see an acquaintance of his brought into ruin or sorrow by the likes of Lord Amundsen.

"And what should I do if Lord Amundsen seeks to dance with me again this evening?" Charity asked, as they made their way across the large room so that they might fetch themselves something to drink. "Should I refuse him?"

"That is entirely your choice," Lady Hayward replied, just as two other ladies turned and, on seeing them, began to draw near. "Lord Amundsen must be discouraged, certainly, but there is no particular need to give him the cut direct. I am sure that, in time, he will understand that there is no eagerness within your heart to draw near to him – if he has not done so already! Still – if you can manage to fill your dance card quickly, before he approaches you..."

Charity nodded slowly, glancing down at her dance card and recalling just how swiftly Lord Amundsen had appeared at the last ball she had attended. He had been on her heels in a few minutes and had written his name down for two dances, including the waltz! She did not want him to do so again, for to be seen waltzing with the very same gentleman at two balls in a row would surely set tongues wagging!

"My dear Lady Hayward, Lady Charity!"

Being quickly drawn into conversation with two of her new acquaintances – a Miss Roberts and her cousin, Miss Stevenson, Charity let her dance card drop from her hand and dangle from the silk ribbon around her wrist. The young ladies' chaperone, Miss Roberts' mother, quickly fell into conversation with Lady Hayward, leaving Charity to speak to the cousins. Laughing and smiling, the two ladies turned quickly and gestured to a small bough which was hung from the ceiling, a few inches above the heads of those who were, at present, dancing.

"Have you seen such a thing before, Lady Charity?" Miss Stevenson asked, as Charity looked at it. "It is a kissing bough!"

Heat instantly rose in Charity's chest.

"A kissing bough?" she repeated, having heard of such a tradition before, but certainly never having once partaken. "Goodness, I did not think that there would be such a thing present!"

The two ladies laughed together, as though Charity was being a little ridiculous.

"But it is to be expected!" exclaimed Miss Roberts, her eyes dancing. "It is near to Christmas Day and so such things will soon be at every ball or soiree that you attend!"

Charity felt her face flush with embarrassment, not wanting to even imagine what she would do if a gentleman she danced with should stop underneath the bough.

"And tis bad luck to refuse a kiss from a gentleman!" Miss Stevenson reminded her, now appearing a trifle more somber. "You cannot do so, Lady Charity, for fear that you will never make a suitable match!"

This, however, was not something that Charity accepted.

"I hardly think that is true," she answered, permitting a smile to cross her lips. "I am not at all likely to accept such a thing from just any gentleman who wishes to take me underneath the bough! I shall be very careful indeed."

This seemed to astonish the two cousins, for they looked at each other with wide eyes, their smiles quickly fading.

"But do you mean to say that you do not *want* such attentions, Lady Charity?" asked Miss Roberts, clearly quite amazed. "I, for one, am very eager indeed to step out to dance, in the hope that a gentleman will be very much inclined to stop under the bough!"

Charity shook her head.

"I confess I am not at all hopeful of such a thing," she replied, a little embarrassed and wondering if her lack of eagerness was to be considered ridiculous. "But I do wish you both every success!"

Miss Stevenson made to say more, only for two gentlemen to approach them and, bowing, asking if they might be able to request a dance from each of the ladies. Having been already acquainted with the gentlemen, Charity had no hesitation in giving them her dance card, and was more than relieved to discover that one Lord Walbridge had secured the waltz for himself. It seemed that Lord Amundsen was not going to be able to take that particular dance, as she had feared.

"Good evening, Lady Charity."

Charity turned quickly and smiled in welcome at Lady Ramsbury.

"Good evening, Lady Ramsbury," she replied, before the lady waved a hand in frustration.

"Come now, Lady Charity, you must not be so formal with me. I think that we are to be considered friends now and thus, you are more than welcome to address me as merely 'Sophia'."

She smiled brightly at Charity who, a little over-whelmed, struggled to find what to say to such a remark. Lady Ramsbury had been very kind to her these first two weeks and Charity had been in her company almost every day – but to be so considered was very pleasant indeed.

"That is very good of you, Lady Ramsbury – I mean, Sophia," Charity replied, her cheeks flushing. "You are more than welcome to call me 'Charity', if you wish to do so." Her heart lifted and she smiled at her friend. "I am very grateful indeed to you for such consideration."

"Think nothing of it," Lady Ramsbury replied, as both Miss Stevenson and Miss Roberts stepped away with the two gentlemen in order to dance. "You are not to dance the cotillion, then?"

Charity shook her head.

"I have not yet been asked," she replied, "but I do not mind particularly. I have other dances that have been taken and, to be quite truthful, Sophia, I have been attempting to avoid Lord Amundsen for fear that he will take the waltz for himself." She glanced down at her dance card. "Not that it can be so now, for it has been taken by another."

Lady Ramsbury frowned, her eyes a little narrowed.

"Lord Amundsen was paying you close attention, I understand," she said, as Charity nodded. "Lord Hosmer was right to speak to Lady Hayward about the fellow. He would *not* have been a good match."

"And yet I fear he is not inclined to give up," Charity answered, her eyes catching a glimpse of the very gentleman they were speaking of, who was standing only a short distance away. For whatever reason – perhaps feeling Charity's gaze upon him, Lord Amundsen looked in their direction, and Charity jerked her head to the right in order to avoid his gaze.

"Now, I fear he is to attend you," Lady Ramsbury muttered, a little darky. "What will you say, should he ask you to dance?"

Charity hesitated, then shrugged one shoulder.

"I shall accept, but only for one dance," she said,

quickly, as Lord Amundsen drew near. "And thereafter, not linger in his company."

"Very wise, Charity," Lady Ramsbury agreed, softly. "Very wise indeed."

Moments later, the gentleman was beside them, and inspecting her dance card.

"This is to be our dance, Lady Charity."

Charity tried to smile as Lord Amundsen came towards her, bowing just a little as he held out his hand.

"But of course, Lord Amundsen," she replied, glancing to Lady Hayward, who gave a small nod, although her eyes remained quite fixed upon Lord Amundsen. "The country dance, is it not?"

He grinned at her, seemingly delighted.

"It is," he replied, as he led her to where the other couples now stood. "It is not my favorite dance, Lady Charity, but your waltz was already taken!"

"Indeed it was," Charity replied, glad when she was able to drop his arm and curtsey, although she was soon back beside him when the music started. Keeping her eyes low and her expression rather vacant, she danced the steps, but showed no interest in permitting a conversation to flow between them.

"And now we are nearing the kissing bough, Lady Charity," she heard Lord Amundsen say, and she felt her eyes widen as her gaze flew to his, seeing the brightness in his expression and the hope that lingered there. "I do hope you will not refuse me!"

Heat climbed up Charity's spine as she faltered in her steps, almost treading on Lord Amundsen's toes and, in the process, making him laugh.

"I fear I shall have to refuse you, for propriety's sake, Lord Amundsen," she said, as he suddenly pulled her near, coming to a sudden stop underneath the bough as the other dancers continued on. "Do forgive me."

"But it will bring you bad luck, Lady Charity," Lord Amundsen cried, holding her gloved hand in his. "Come now, it will mean nothing at all. Everyone in the *beau monde* is aware that the kissing bough holds no significance." He drew a little nearer and Charity tried to step back, only to realize just how tightly he held her hand. The look on his face was turning into something of a leer and Charity could not help but feel afraid, looking up at him and finding her heart quickening with a great and sudden anxiety.

"My hand, if you please," she stammered, attempting to lift it. "A kiss to my hand is more than acceptable and will certainly push aside any bad luck that might follow!"

Lord Amundsen chuckled and another thrill of fear ran down Charity's spine. The music seemed to take on a somber tone, the notes murky and dark as she looked into Lord Amundsen's eyes and saw the determination there. She knew precisely what he sought and found herself all the more reluctant to give it, beginning to fear that she would be forced into a situation where she might then struggle to remove herself from his embrace entirely. Was that his intention? Did he think to kiss her in such a way that an engagement would *have* to be secured between them?"

"Amundsen." Charity practically wilted with relief as Lord Hosmer appeared, stepping out of the crowd and coming towards them. "Lady Charity does not look well,"

Lord Hosmer continued, his tone not at all angry but rather an expression of concern written across his face. "Lady Charity, do permit me to escort you back to Lady Hayward. I am sure that you will feel much more yourself once you sit down and rest for a short time."

Lord Amundsen opened his mouth to protest, to perhaps state that he was well able to do such a thing on his own, but given that his grip had loosened significantly on her hand, Charity was able to pull it free from his and step back at once.

"Thank you, Lord Hosmer," she murmured, quickly accepting the offer of his arm and no longer able to even glance up at Lord Amundsen. "Excuse me, Lord Amundsen. I do feel a little faint."

Praying that she had not garnered too much attention from either the other dancers or the guests who looked on, Charity tried to steady her breathing as Lord Hosmer led her quickly towards where Lady Hayward was waiting, seeing her chaperone's face white and drawn.

"I am quite all right," Charity said quickly, as Lady Hayward grasped her hand tightly and Lord Hosmer stepped back, his duty done. "Lord Amundsen was quite... determined to steal a kiss from me."

"I do not think that was all he intended," Lord Hosmer replied, grimly. "He is nothing but a scoundrel, Lady Charity, and I should advise you not to step out to dance with him again."

Charity nodded, relieved when Lady Hayward's grip on her hand began to loosen.

"I shall not do so," she answered, firmly. "I thank you again, Lord Hosmer, for your awareness of the situation and your help. I cannot even imagine what might have occurred if you had not..."

She trailed off, her throat suddenly constricting as visions of what could have happened began to fill her thoughts.

"Think nothing of it," Lord Hosmer said and, with a quick bow, then turned from her and made his way across the room.

Charity watched him for a moment before letting out a long breath and trying to smile at Lady Hayward.

"I am quite all right," she promised, for what was now the second time. "Truly I am, Lady Hayward."

"I should never have suggested that you dance with Lord Amundsen again," Lady Hayward said, shaking her head. "That was very foolish of me."

"It was not to be expected that he would attempt to do such a thing," Charity replied, not wanting Lady Hayward to take on blame that was not her own. "The kissing bough is present and many gentlemen, I see, are stopping beneath it. Although most are behaving with propriety, taking the hand of the lady and lifting it to their lips." She watched as another gentleman and lady stopped beneath it, doing precisely as she had just said. "Lord Amundsen's motives were, I believe, entirely unscrupulous." With another long breath, Charity put a smile on her face which, given Lady Hayward's doubtful expression, she did not instantly believe. "I will be more than happy to remain and to dance with the other gentlemen on my card. To leave now would not, I believe, be wise."

Lady Hayward studied Charity carefully for some minutes, then, eventually, nodded.

"Very well," she agreed, quietly. "But Lord Amundsen is not even to be recognized any longer, Lady Charity. We *shall* give him the cut direct and, if anyone should ask, I will be glad to inform them of the reason for it."

Charity nodded without hesitation.

"I quite agree."

"And I believe that it would be good to speak again to Lord Hosmer, to thank him for all that he has done," Lady Hayward continued. "I know he will be reluctant but I –"

"That is my thought precisely," Charity agreed, softly. "I should be very glad to do so, Lady Hayward. If he had not noticed, then a great deal of harm might have come about."

Before Lady Hayward could reply, Lady Ramsbury came to join them, her eyes a little wide.

"I have heard from Lord Hosmer what occurred with Lord Amundsen!" she exclaimed, her hand on Charity's arm. "You are quite all right?"

"I am," Charity replied, softly, quickly giving an account of what had happened and Lord Hosmer's intervention. "I do wish very much to thank Lord Hosmer again for his willingness to assist me, as he did. Although to do so this evening would not suffice, for I am sure he will simply brush it off as though it is entirely unimportant."

Lady Ramsbury nodded.

"Then you must come to take tea tomorrow and we

will discuss the matter at length – and I shall make certain that Lord Hosmer is present also," she stated, firmly. "You will both be able to attend?"

Charity glanced at Lady Hayward, who nodded.

"Yes, of course," she replied, gratefully. "Thank you, Sophia."

CHAPTER SIX

"I hear you saved a certain young lady from difficulty last evening."

Benedict grimaced and looked away, choosing not to say anything. Last evening, he had noticed, only by chance, that Lord Amundsen was standing underneath the kissing bough with Lady Charity, and that she appeared to be in distress. There was nothing more than that to his attempt to help her and he did not much like the knowing look on Ramsbury's face.

"I would commend you for your actions, if it was not for the look of frustration on your face," Ramsbury continued, as Lady Ramsbury chuckled, hiding her mouth with her hand. "You do not appear to be at all glad that you did such an excellent thing."

"I do not need to discuss it, that is all," Benedict replied, gruffly. "It was not a significant matter."

"I believe that Lady Hayward would not agree," Lady Ramsbury stated, only for there to come a knock at the door. Rising, the lady smiled back at him. "And I believe that now, you will be able to hear such a thing for yourself!"

A little confused, Benedict rose to his feet, only to see Lady Hayward and Lady Charity step into the room. His brow furrowed even though he bowed to greet them, beginning to think that Lord and Lady Ramsbury had deliberately arranged this particular meeting so that he would have to speak to Lady Charity. He prayed that they were not attempting to encourage any sort of intimacy between himself and Lady Charity, for that was, he was quite sure, something he had stated would not be occurring, no matter how much his friends might wish it!

"I am so very glad to see you, Lady Charity," Lady Ramsbury said, as the young lady rose from her curtsey. "And you are quite well? You are not overly upset from last evening?"

"I am not upset in the least," Lady Charity replied, just as Benedict made to sit back down. "Oh, Lord Hosmer, might I speak with you quietly for a few moments?" She glanced to the back of the room. "Just over here?"

Benedict swallowed hard, finding himself nodding before he had even decided to agree. Lady Hayward appeared quite at ease with the situation, which surprised him, given that it was not particularly proper for a young lady of quality to speak privately with a gentleman, even if they were within the same room as other people. And yet, his legs took him to Lady Charity as she moved across the room towards the large windows, feeling the slight coolness rub at his cheeks as they stepped away from the roaring fire.

"Lord Hosmer." Lady Charity turned to look at him directly, as a burst of laughter came from Lord Ramsbury and Lady Hayward. "I wanted very much to speak to you about last evening."

Benedict cleared his throat, his hands behind his back.

"There is no need to do so," he replied, as Lady Charity shook her head. "I am only glad that –"

"It meant a very great deal," Lady Charity interrupted, before he could finish. "I do not think that you are fully aware of the gravity of the situation, Lord Hosmer. Lord Amundsen, I believe, was attempting to force a match between us. The look on his face when he stood before me and practically demanded...."

She trailed off, clearly unable to finish speaking, the last few words strained and tight.

Benedict felt his heart twist in his chest.

"I am only glad that I was able to do so, Lady Charity," he said, gently, no longer as irritated as before. "As I was saying to Ramsbury only a few minutes ago, it was just by sheer luck that I saw you and Lord Amundsen. I could tell from the look on your face that he was pressing his advantage." He shook his head, feeling a trace of anger begin to burn in his heart. "Lord Amundsen is not a gentleman, nor ought to be considered as one. I am sorry that he treated you so."

"There must be something I can do to show you my gratitude," Lady Charity said, after a few moments, her voice no longer strained. "Some way that I can aid you, as you have aided me."

Shaking his head, Benedict held up his hands.

"There is no need for you to do so, Lady Charity, truly."

She looked back at him, considering.

"I do not think I will accept such a statement from you, Lord Hosmer," she said, quietly. "I will do what I can to encourage you, mayhap?"

A small gleam came into her eye but Benedict only frowned.

"I do not know what you mean."

"It appears that you find London most melancholy," she replied, spreading her hands. "Perhaps I should make it my duty to encourage you to find a little more enjoyment, in the hope that this will lift your spirits."

A flicker of worry snapped across Benedict's forehead.

"There is no need, Lady Charity," he said, firmly. "I am quite contented, truly."

"What is this?"

Ramsbury's voice carried across the room to where Benedict and Lady Charity were speaking.

"Did I hear you say that you are *contented*, Hosmer?"

Benedict opened his mouth to state that there was no need for Ramsbury to listen to his conversation, only for Lady Charity to respond.

"Yes, Lord Ramsbury, that is precisely what Lord Hosmer has stated," she said, with a small frown. "Do you mean to say that you do not believe it to be so?"

At this, Ramsbury let out a guffaw of laughter with Lady Ramsbury laughing quietly also. Lady Charity, clearly interested in what they both had to say about the matter, drew nearer so that she might continue the conversation – whereas Benedict remained precisely where he was.

"Might I ask what brought this discussion about?" Ramsbury asked, as Lady Charity sat down in a chair near Lady Ramsbury. "Surely Hosmer did not tell you as much simply out of his own free will?"

Lady Charity cast a quick glance back towards Benedict and Benedict grimaced, wishing that he had the authority to demand that she say nothing.

"I – I was offering to encourage Lord Hosmer to greater cheer during his time in London, in whatever way I can," Lady Charity replied, speaking a little tentatively. "Given what he has done to save my reputation, I thought it only fair to attempt to repay his kindness in some way."

"That is very good of you, Charity," Lady Ramsbury said, throwing a quick glance towards Benedict. "Lord Hosmer told you, however, that he has no need of such encouragements, because he is so very contented at present?"

The incredulous sound to her voice made Benedict wince and he looked away, having no desire to go and sit near to them at all.

"He did," Lady Charity replied, casting an uncertain look towards Benedict. "I – I sought only to be of aid in some way, in recompense for both of the times that Lord Hosmer has assisted me with Lord Amundsen. If Lord Hosmer is truly contented, as he has said, then then I am more than willing to accept such a thing."

Ramsbury chuckled, a broad smile spreading across his face. Benedict willed him not to say a word, silently begged him to remain quiet, but it was of little use. Ramsbury was already speaking.

"Lady Charity, I will tell you quite openly that Hosmer is not at all contented," he said, one eyebrow lifting in an almost superior manner. "I will not state why, but I am quite certain that, with your own awareness of Hosmer's behavior, you must struggle to accept such a statement from him!"

Benedict glowered at his friend, now praying that Lady Hayward would step in and state that such a suggestion, whilst well meant by Lady Charity, was not required and that they might as well leave the matter alone. However, one look towards Lady Hayward, and Benedict realized that she was quite enjoying the conversation, seemingly just as interested in what Ramsbury was saying as Lady Charity herself!

"I – I do not know what to think, Lord Ramsbury," Lady Charity replied, clearly a little awkward now as she folded her hands in her lap and dared another glance towards him. "But I should not pry, of course."

Lady Ramsbury held up both hands.

"Of course, of course you should not pry, and it is clear that you are not doing so either," she replied, a twinkle in her eye. "But Lord Hosmer ought to be very careful indeed of speaking such untruths amongst friends!" She laughed at Benedict's hard gaze, ignoring the clear frustration in his expression. "I am certain that Lord Hosmer is not at all contented, Lady Charity, and I am all the more certain that anything you can do to improve his time here in London will be gladly accepted." Her eyes turned back to Benedict, as though daring him to disagree. "Although, Lady Charity, I think that you have a very difficult task ahead of you!"

Benedict did not know what to say. He wanted to throw up his hands, to demand that Lord and Lady Ramsbury stop their nonsense and leave him to himself, just as he had asked Ramsbury to do, so many times. But yet, something restrained him. Lady Charity was, Benedict realized, attempting to be generous in both spirit and in action and she was doing so solely in an attempt to show gratitude for his kindness. Try as he might, he could not see any clear way for him to refuse such a thing, not when Lord and Lady Ramsbury were clearly so eager and when Lady Hayward was present also. To do so would appear to be churlish and a little rude – something he did not want to display towards Lady Charity.

"Truly, Lady Charity, there is no particular need," he found himself saying, as Lady Charity turned to look at him. "You are very kind indeed to wish to repay me in such a way but I am being very truthful indeed when I state that I am quite contented as I am." His lips curved in a rueful smile. "Contented in my melancholy."

"Which, I must say, is growing a little tiresome," Ramsbury chuckled, making Lady Charity flush – although whether from humor or embarrassment, Benedict did not know. "Lady Charity, I shall be very pleased indeed if you can manage to improve Hosmer's demeanor although, as my wife has said, I think it will prove to be very difficult indeed!"

"Then I shall be glad to try," Lady Charity replied, no longer looking towards Benedict who, feeling rather defeated, flopped down into a chair and looked about to see if there was any brandy to hand. "So long as you have no objections, Lord Hosmer?"

Benedict turned his head to look at Lady Charity. There was a slight hesitation in her expression, her hazel eyes swirling with clouds that sparkled with browns and greens. Lady Hayward was not making any particular protest, Benedict noted, for she sat quietly and waited for his response, clearly quite contented with the discussion that was taking place at present. He drew in a long breath, resigned to the fact that he would not be able to protest or refuse in these current circumstances. His only hope would be to very quickly ensure that Lady Charity realized just how much he was disinclined towards the idea and that she might very soon give up.

"No objections at all, Lady Charity," he answered, with a heavy sigh following his words. "Although I shall repeat again that I am quite contented, just as I am."

Ramsbury snorted at this and, within a few minutes, the conversation then turned to Lord Amundsen. Benedict said nothing of importance, choosing instead simply to listen and to consider, quietly, what he might say to Lord and Lady Ramsbury when the time came. He would make it quite clear to them both that he did not appreciate their input, or their encouragement of Lady Charity, and he would demand that they do all they could to set her away from that path. He could only hope that they would agree.

GIVEN that it was a very cold day indeed – although

certainly dry – Benedict did not expect anyone else to be walking through Hyde Park on a freezing winter's afternoon. He had chosen to do so, however, for the idea of being alone at home with his thoughts had not been an encouraging one. Ever since Lady Charity had spoken to him of her desire to encourage him from whatever it was that troubled him so, he had been unable to think of anything else. That had been some three days ago and still, he felt himself quite tormented.

Of course, Lady Charity had only been encouraged by Lord and Lady Ramsbury and, had it not been for them, he might have been able to dissuade her. His explanation, his frustration and his repeated desire that they step back and suggest that Lady Charity no longer attempt such a thing had been met with outright refusal, much to his own annoyance. Lady Charity had not, as yet, done anything other than converse with him when she could, but he could see the questions in her eyes whenever she looked at him. It was as though she wanted desperately to discover the truth about his melancholy, about his dislike of the Christmas season, and yet her interest made him all the more determined to remain silent.

"Good afternoon, Lord Hosmer. It is a very cold day, is it not?"

Benedict looked up, his gaze having rested on the path before him rather than straight ahead. Given that he had not thought that there would be anyone else present, he had been wandering slowly through the park, taking his time and ignoring the cold which had begun to nip at his toes.

"It is," he replied, looking into the faces of Lady Hayward, Lady Charity and another he did not recognize. "I do beg your pardon if I was walking into your path."

Lady Charity smiled at him and Benedict could not help but notice the pink in her cheeks and the sparkle in her eyes. The cold seemed to only add to her beauty – although he, of course, grew irritated with himself that he had even noticed such a thing.

"You were not," she assured him, warmly. "Are you fond of taking walks in the park during very cold days, Lord Hosmer?"

One corner of his mouth lifted.

"It depends very much on the day, Lady Charity," he answered. "If it is raining or hailing or snowing – as it is inclined to do this time of year – then you will find me sitting comfortably at home and being more than contented with a roaring fire."

Lady Hayward cleared her throat gently.

"Forgive me for interrupting, but I should like to introduce you to Lady Riverland. She is a dear friend of mine and I have been very glad to see her again." She continued on with the introductions and Benedict bowed, expressing his gladness with meeting such a lady. Thereafter, he lifted his head and looked directly at the path ahead of him, wondering how he was going to be able to remove himself from their company and continue on his way. "We are to return to our carriage, I think," Lady Hayward said, just as Benedict had been about to excuse himself. "It is very cold, and both myself and Lady Riverland find the air very chilled." A small shiver captured her frame even as she smiled at him. "Might you be willing to accompany Lady Charity to the carriage, Lord Hosmer? As you can see, Lady Riverland and I are walking together and I do fear that Lady Charity might slip if she has no-one beside her, for the frost still coats some of these paths."

Benedict took a moment to look into Lady Hayward's eyes, but saw nothing of mischief or trickery there. It appeared that she was rather concerned for Lady Charity and eager to make certain that they all returned to their carriage safely – and given that he had been requested to do such a thing, Benedict knew that it would not be gentlemanly for him to refuse.

"But of course," he replied, inclining his head as a look of relief flooded Lady Hayward's face. "Lead on, Lady Hayward."

Lady Charity's face was now a rosier pink than before, although she accepted his arm without hesitation.

"Forgive Lady Hayward's forwardness, I beg you," she said, softly. "Lady Riverland has already stumbled and I believe that it startled them both very badly."

A forced smile was brought to Benedict's lips.

"I quite understand," he replied, a little tightly. "There is no need to worry, Lady Charity. I will be glad to return you to the carriage."

Lady Charity lapsed into silence for some minutes as they walked slowly back towards the entrance of the park. Their pace was dictated by that of the ladies in front of them and, upon occasion, Benedict had to bite his lip in frustration at the slowness of their steps.

"I must ask, Lord Hosmer, whether or not you would

be truly glad of my company and willingness to bring a little more happiness to you," Lady Charity said suddenly, her face turning towards him. "I have the distinct impression that you believed Lord and Lady Ramsbury to be very forward in their remarks when last we discussed things." Biting her lip for a moment, she searched his eyes with her own. "I should not like to importune you."

A little surprised that she had spoken so openly and with such discernment, Benedict allowed himself a small smile.

"You do not importune me, Lady Charity," he found himself saying. "It is entirely the doing of Lord and Lady Ramsbury. They believe that such an encouragement would be good for me."

"But you are contented with your despondency and your unhappiness at present?" she asked, surprising him all the more. "I should like to know why you feel such sorrow at this particular time of year – a time when I find nothing but happiness and joy – but as I have stated before, I will not pry."

Benedict let out a long breath, pushing away any tension that he felt.

"I am grateful to you for that," he answered, "for I shall not state as much to you, Lady Charity."

"Then I suppose I shall have to continue on as was agreed," came the swift reply. "Given that you have said my actions would not plague you in any way, there appears to be no reason for me not to do so." Again, there came a protest to his lips which was not spoken. Benedict found himself struggling to find the right response, determined to tell her that he did not want such a thing but yet unable to force himself to say it. It was a most extraordinary feeling and one that Benedict did not find agreeable at all. "And now you have returned me to the carriage." Lady Charity let go of his arm, turned and smiled at him, before dropping her gaze and bobbing a quick curtsy. "I thank you, Lord Hosmer. Good afternoon."

Lady Hayward thanked him also, then climbed quickly into the carriage, which pulled away almost immediately. Benedict was left standing near the park gate, watching it depart and realizing, with a very heavy heart, that he would not be rid of Lady Charity's good nature any time soon.

CHAPTER SEVEN

C harity smiled at Lady Hayward as she came into the room to join her for a warming cup of afternoon tea. The day was very cold indeed and the hail had been driving hard at the windows for many hours. They had no intention of setting foot out of doors this afternoon and certainly, Charity did not expect any afternoon callers to arrive either!

"I am sure we shall have snow," Lady Hayward declared, as she sat down in a chair near the fire. "With Christmas Day only a fortnight away, I believe that we shall have a very cold day indeed!"

The smile on Charity's face did not fade.

"I do not think I should mind that," she answered, speaking truthfully. "For it is not the weather that makes the day but the company."

Lady Hayward smiled happily.

"That is very true indeed," she answered, softly. "I do hope that you will not mind too much about being away from your father and sisters for Christmas Day. My own family will be present but, besides that, we will attend Lord and Lady Ramsbury's dinner and, I am sure, spend the best part of the day there." Her smile grew. "And Lord Hosmer will be there also, although whether or not he will still have that particular sullenness about him, even on this happiest of days, I cannot imagine!"

A chuckle escaped from Charity as she imagined the festive scene, where they were all sitting around the table, enjoying good company, excellent food and the joy that came with Christmas Day, only for Lord Hosmer to remain seated in the corner, his expression dull and his eyes flat.

"I am certain that even Lord Hosmer could not remain so, not when he would be surrounded by such happiness and joy," she answered, although Lady Hayward shook her head. "There must be something that brings him contentment, surely?!"

A light flickered in Lady Hayward's eyes.

"That will be for you to find out, Lady Charity," she answered, reminding Charity of what she had agreed to. "That is, if you still wish to do so. From Lord Hosmer's expression, I am sure that he would be quite contented if you chose not to do so."

Inwardly, Charity sighed, although she did not allow it to escape from her lips. It was practically impossible for her to explain – to the point that she did not even attempt to do so, even to herself! She knew very well that Lord Hosmer did not want her to seek out his troubles, to encourage him and to attempt to bring him a little more happiness, but for whatever reason, she could not give up the idea. When it had been discussed with Lord and

Lady Ramsbury, they had been so very eager that Charity had been more than a little intrigued as to why Lord Hosmer appeared so disillusioned, so melancholy and miserable. She had not, of course, asked any questions nor attempted to discover the truth by alternative means, but there was now a small flame of determination lit within her heart. She would, in time, find out the root cause of Lord Hosmer's dislike of the Christmas season and would show him that there was still joy to be found in it.

"You are determined, however."

"I am," Charity answered, quietly, although she did not see nor hear any reproach in Lady Hayward's voice or expression. "I would refrain, however, if you wish it?"

Lady Hayward considered for a moment and then shook her head.

"I think, Lady Charity, that Lord Hosmer might make you an excellent match," she said, surprising Charity greatly. "I know that there is no such willingness on his part to even consider an acquaintance which might become something more than only that, but if you are determined to follow through with what has been suggested, then I would expect there to come a little more of a closeness between you." She arched one eyebrow and instantly, Charity felt a flush of heat climb up her spine. "You have not considered the idea?"

"N-no," Charity stammered, rather taken aback at the idea. "Lord Hosmer is handsome, certainly, but his character is so very...." She trailed off, trying to find the right words. "He is so very downhearted all of the time that I find the idea of even considering such a thing to be not worth even a moment's consideration!"

Lady Hayward sighed and spread her hands.

"You find him handsome at least," she said, a small, teasing smile adding to the twinkle in her eyes. "Then, what I will say, Lady Charity, is that you should not lose yourself in this affair. If you are not to consider Lord Hosmer in such a light, if you do not think that there is any possibility of a connection between you, then do not permit yourself to become entirely wrapped up in this matter, for fear that you might lose an opportunity with another gentleman." She hesitated, the smile fading from her lips. "Do you understand what I am trying to say? I fear that I have explained myself poorly."

Charity shook her head.

"You have not done so, Lady Hayward," she answered. "I quite understand. I am here in London to seek out a decent match. To become too caught up with Lord Hosmer might mean that I miss other gentlemen who could be precisely what I am seeking." Nodding to herself slowly, Charity was aware of the uncomfortable sensation in her heart. "I quite understand. I will be very careful indeed."

"Be aware of what is going on within your heart, Lady Charity," came the surprising reply. "You may well be careful in your dealings with Lord Hosmer, but should things change in terms of how you see him, how you view him and the like, then I must ask you to permit yourself time to consider it all very carefully indeed."

Charity did not immediately respond, finding that the strange, uncomfortable feeling in her heart was entirely to do with the idea of stepping away from Lord Hosmer and setting her attention on another. There was something about the gentleman which was very captivating indeed, but was that simply the mystery which surrounded him? When she discovered the truth, would she be able to step away from him without any concern? Or would she find herself all the more enthralled by him, once they had drawn that little bit nearer to each other?

"Lady Charity?"

"Yes, Lady Hayward," Charity said quickly, realizing that, as yet, she had not said a word. "I will do as you suggest, although I must state that I do not believe there could be such a change."

She tried to smile but could tell it faltered. Lady Hayward's smile was a knowing one and, whilst she nodded and then rose to ring the bell for tea, Charity knew very well that her chaperone was all too aware of Charity's innermost thoughts. For whatever reason, Lady Hayward seemed to be able to see what Charity was hiding deep within her heart and was able, already, to foresee what might occur. Whether that was unsettling or encouraging, Charity did not know.

"When are you to see Lord Hosmer again?"

"This evening, I believe, at Lord and Lady Bollington's soiree," came the quick reply, as Charity prayed now that the discussion might move to something else. "I thought to wear one of my new gowns."

"An excellent idea!" Lady Hayward exclaimed, finally allowing Charity to discuss something other than Lord Hosmer. And yet, no matter what they spoke of, no matter what they said, there was always that gentle tug at the back of her mind, that pressing of her heart that now seemed quite impossible to remove.

She would see Lord Hosmer again tonight.

"I do hope you enjoy the evening."

Charity thanked their hosts and, alongside Lady Hayward, made her way towards the center of the room where a few other ladies were conversing. She was doing her best not to look for Lord Hosmer, not to allow her eyes to flit from one place to the next as she searched for him. It would not be wise to do so and certainly might bring her a little embarrassment, should anyone notice that she was not paying them and their conversation the correct amount of attention and interest.

"Good evening, Lady Hayward, Lady Charity!"

Charity quickly bobbed a curtsy.

"Good evening, Lord Ramsbury, Lady Ramsbury." She laughed as Lady Ramsbury's eyes narrowed in playful reminder. "I mean, good evening Sophia."

"Ah!" Lord Ramsbury exclaimed, as the smile returned to Lady Ramsbury's face. "So she has you calling her by her forename name then, does she?" He twinkled at his wife, who reached across to squeeze his arm. "That seems quite suitable, given that you are such close acquaintances."

"Lady Hayward and I were just discussing Christmas Day," Charity replied, as Lady Ramsbury nodded. "We are both very much looking forward to joining you." She could not pretend that there was not a small stab of pain at the thought of not being present with her sisters and her father for Christmas Day but, as she reminded herself, such changes must take place if she was ever to wed. She would have to become used to not being at home with the only family she had ever known and, instead, set up her own life and her own situation with happiness and eagerness. "You are both very kind to have invited us."

"Oh, but it will be marvelous!" Lady Ramsbury exclaimed, clasping her hands together tightly in front of her. "We are so looking forward to having you both join us." She laughed suddenly, looking to her husband. "And we shall not be burdened with only Lord Hosmer's company who, I can assure you, does nothing other than remain rather sullen throughout the entire day! Unless," she continued, throwing a quick smile towards Charity, "you are able to improve his manner by then, Charity."

"I fear you might well be a little too hopeful, Sophia," Charity replied, laughing, only to see Lord Hosmer standing just a few steps away from them all, near the very back of the room. He was holding a glass of brandy in one hand and his eyes were roving across the room, studying each person for only a moment. His lips were pulled tight, a hardness about his expression and a darkness in his eyes which Charity had not seen before. Her smile faded as a stone dropped into her stomach. Was something wrong? Was it the fact that *she* was present which made him appear so?

"Charity?"

Charity caught herself and looked back at Lady Ramsbury, who was watching her with a concerned expression.

"I am quite all right," she answered, quickly. "'Tis

only that Lord Hosmer is present this evening and appears to be most upset about something." She gestured carefully towards him, not wanting to be seen to be doing so. "I can only hope that it is not my presence which has done such a thing!"

Lady Ramsbury glanced at her husband, a worried expression on her face, before she pasted a quick smile on her lips and shook her head.

"No, indeed not, Charity. It is not your presence which has done so," she said, with such a confidence that Charity found herself wanting to believe her. "Why do you not go and speak with him for a few moments? You will see his expression change in an instant, I am sure."

Charity hesitated, glancing to Lady Hayward who, with a tiny nod, assured her that, should she wish to do so, then she would be quite in line with propriety given that both Lady Ramsbury and Lady Hayward would be able to observe her. It took a few moments for Charity to decide to approach him, however, for the expression on his face was still rather foreboding and, despite Lady Ramsbury's assurances, she did not feel particularly confident.

"Lord Hosmer?"

Her feet had carried her towards him before she had even consciously made her decision to do so. Her voice quavered just a little and Charity flushed with embarrassment as his eyes shot towards her, holding that same hardness she had seen only moments before.

"Lady Charity." Lord Hosmer bowed then cleared his throat. "Good evening."

"Good evening."

She did not know what else to say, her throat constricting as she looked back at him, wondering what it was she was doing coming to speak to him so. It was foolishness, was it not, given that he most likely did not want her company?

"Did you feel sorrow for my loneliness and thought to come to speak to me?"

Charity blinked in surprise, looking back at Lord Hosmer and taking in the tightness of his jaw and the way his lips flattened all the more.

"Lord Hosmer?"

"Did you see me standing alone and think to come and encourage me in some way?" he asked, a little more tightly. "I assure you, Lady Charity, there is no need. I am quite contented in my own company."

"You have spoken of being so contented before," she reminded him, as gently as she could. "And perhaps this time, *I* am the one who does not believe your words."

Steeling herself, she looked into his face and held his angry gaze, feeling as though such anger was being directed solely towards her, without any true understanding as to why that should be.

"Perhaps I do not wish for company."

His words were stinging and Charity felt herself recoil inwardly, only to draw in a long breath and force herself to speak with both determination and courage.

"Then why did you attend the soiree?" she asked, as he narrowed his eyes just a little. "If you were very contented in your own company, if you were glad to be standing alone, then for what purpose did you attend this evening? Surely you knew that there would be others present, others who might wish to converse and the like?"

Lord Hosmer's jaw worked for a few moments until, finally, he dropped his head and she heard a heavy sigh escape from him.

"You are quite correct, Lady Charity," he told her, much to her surprise. "It was foolish to attend when I was quite happy with my own company. However, perhaps a part of me hoped to find good conversation and perhaps a game of cards where I might forget all my troubles." He grimaced, lifting his head as he did so. "As yet, the card game has not started but I can assure you that I will be in attendance the moment it begins."

"I see," Charity murmured, feeling now a little embarrassed. It was clear that Lord Hosmer did not appreciate nor want her company. The only thing he sought was, it seemed, a game of cards where he might remain entirely silent and concentrate only on the matter at hand. "Then if you are so contented and do not wish me to remain, I shall return to Lady Hayward. Forgive me for attempting to do as I have promised."

To her astonishment, Lord Hosmer's hand shot out and grasped her wrist, preventing her from turning away from him and making her way back to Lady Hayward. It was gone from her in a moment but the pressure of his fingers on her wrist seemed to remain.

"Forgive me, Lady Charity," Lord Hosmer said, more gently now. "I have been rather rude, have I not?"

"Yes," she stated, without hesitation. "Yes, Lord Hosmer, you have."

"And you are only doing what I know to be a kind

attempt at removing this darkness from my expression and my soul," he continued, as Charity looked back at him steadily. "As I have said, Lady Charity, I fear that you will not succeed in this and that, time and again, I shall disappoint you."

Charity shook her head, looking at him and finding his open expression, his evident willingness to now speak to her, to be one that did not push her away but did, in fact, encourage her somewhat.

"You have not disappointed me, Lord Hosmer," she told him, firmly. "In fact, I should say that my attempts have been successful, given that there is now no longer the anger in your eyes, the hardness in your expression nor the irritation in your voice." She smiled at him and, much to her astonishment, there came an easy smile back from him in return. "I shall count myself quite effective, in fact."

Lord Hosmer said nothing for a moment or two, his eyes searching hers as he looked into her face. It was as though he was thinking hard about what she had said, about what she had suggested, and now was deciding whether or not to agree with her.

"You have distracted me, certainly," he said, slowly. "That, I suppose, is a good thing."

Charity lifted one eyebrow.

"Distracted you, Lord Hosmer?"

He sighed again and ran one hand over his eyes.

"There is a matter, Lady Charity, that has not left my heart nor my soul these last few years," he told her, making Charity's heart quicken as she realized just how openly he was speaking to her. "It was at this very time of year, just before Christmas, that all that I believed, all that I hoped for, was taken from me in an instant. And, at times, I am unfortunately in the same room as someone who was present at that time." Closing his eyes, Lord Hosmer shook his head and Charity saw his jaw working hard for a few moments, as though he were attempting to keep his expression calm but struggling very hard to do so. "I should be able to forget it all, of course. I should be able to simply greet them and then continue on regardless, but it is not so. The pain is still present, Lady Charity. The anger still burns in my heart. And thus, I do not feel as though you shall ever succeed, for my own heart will not let me be at ease."

Charity stared back at him as he lifted his head and opened his eyes, and she felt as though he had taken a great burden from his back, swung it down to the floor between them and had then revealed it to her. There were no particular details, of course, but finally, she had been told precisely *why* Lord Hosmer appeared to be so disillusioned with everything here in London. It was because he still carried a weight with him, a weight that burdened his very soul and brought him low. It was not something she could understand fully but, at the very least, there was the awareness now that he was not simply melancholy for the sake of it. Finally, she knew why he struggled so – and her heart opened towards him with both sympathy and compassion.

"Is that not all the more reason for me to be willing to encourage you, Lord Hosmer?" she asked, eventually. "You speak of pain and distress and an inability to free yourself from it – but what if you simply have not had the aid that you need to do so? What if I am able to encourage you in such a way that this darkness departs from you?"

Lord Hosmer's lips twisted in a sad smile.

"But Lady Charity, you must consider the fact that mayhap I myself am not willing to allow such things to pass from my heart and mind," he told her, making her frown. "I am perhaps not as willing nor as eager as you to forget about such things."

"But why would you not wish to?" she asked, as Lord Hosmer held up one hand and shook his head.

"I have no wish to discuss matters," he said, in such a firm tone that Charity knew at once that she would have no opportunity to speak to him further on the subject. "I do hope that you will not take offence, Lady Charity, but there is the truth. I have shared with you something of my burden – but it is a burden that is not yet ready to leave my shoulders." His eyes searched hers, a gentler expression now drifting across his features. "I only hope that you can understand."

"I will not give up," she said, determinedly. "I –"

Her attention was suddenly caught by something in the window, which, to her surprise, still had the drapes pulled back from it. Something moved again and Charity caught her breath, a bright smile pulling at her lips as she realized what it was.

"Come, Lord Hosmer," she said, reaching out to catch his arm and turning him, bodily, towards the window which was only a few steps away. "Come and I will show you a little happiness. A little joy." Lord Hosmer grunted but came willingly, allowing Charity to lead him towards the window, her hand still on his sleeve. She glanced back at Lady Hayward, making certain that her chaperone could still see her, relieved when the lady nodded and smiled. She turned her attention back to the window. "Look, Lord Hosmer," she said, softly. "Even with your struggle and your burden, do you not find even the slightest bit of joy in seeing the snow fall?" Charity watched it for some minutes, finding herself transfixed by the scene before her. There was something so beautiful about the snow gently falling on the streets of London; the white flakes gently caught by the lantern light. Without realizing she was still holding Lord Hosmer's arm, Charity let out a long, contented breath and pressed her free hand to her heart. "It always makes me very glad to see it."

Lord Hosmer cleared his throat and shattered the quietness of the moment, making Charity look up at him sharply, her attention suddenly returned to him rather than to the snow.

"I am afraid that even the snow will not permit me to loosen my burden at all, Lady Charity," he said, gruffly. "It is not something that I find any enjoyment in."

"But how can that be?" Charity asked, rather taken aback at the remark. "There is such a gentle beauty in the snow falling that surely it must touch your heart!"

"It does not," came the hard reply, with Lord Hosmer frowning so heavily that Charity caught her breath. "Rather it reminds me of the cruel way that the happiness I had thought would be mine for the rest of my days was taken from me." His eyes glinted as he looked directly back into her eyes. "The snow was falling then too, Lady Charity. Every year, it reminds me of that moment."

Charity drew in a steadying breath, lifting her chin and refusing to be cowed by Lord Hosmer's dark depression.

"Then might I recommend, Lord Hosmer, that you find a new memory to cover over that particular one?" she suggested, placing both hands on her hips. "If you seek out the sorrowful memories, then you will, of course, become trapped in misery."

"I do not seek them out," he stated, his eyes a little narrowed as he appeared to glare at her. "They are already there, waiting for me."

Refusing to give in to his anger, to bow to his clear irritation, Charity took a small step closer to him and immediately saw his expression shift. His eyes widened – as though he had not expected her to move so close to him, had not thought that she would challenge him in such a way – and the anger quickly faded from his expression.

"Then do not permit it entry, Lord Hosmer," she said quietly, knowing that to speak with gentleness and understanding was of great importance at present. "You must choose to set it from you, must choose to force it to depart. Instead, find something a little happier to consider so that you might look out at the snow and find a contentment there. Else I fear that you shall never see the beauty that is before you."

Quite how long they stood there together, Charity did not know. She had nothing more to say and so had simply looked up into his face and held his gaze quite steadily, astonished when he had done the same. There was no frustration in his expression, no upset nor anger. Instead, there was a slight frown dancing across his brow and questions in his eyes that she dared not even consider answering.

His hand suddenly touched hers and Charity's breath hitched as she looked down, realizing that, through this entire conversation, she had not once let go of his sleeve. Now his free hand was atop her own and she let go of his sleeve at once, only to find his hand lingering on hers.

"Mayhap you are right, Lady Charity," he said, his tone no longer gruff or irritated. "I – I had not considered such a thing." His frown deepened. "Mayhap I have been so caught up in my memories that I have become quite used to them. Perhaps I now expect them to arrive, to spoil whatever else is occurring around me." Shaking his head, he let out a long breath and finally released her hand. Charity pulled it back at once, all too aware of the creeping warmth that ran up her hand and into her arm. "You have given me something to think on, Lady Charity."

"I – I am glad," she replied, noting the quaver in her voice and finding herself a little embarrassed by it. "I do truly want to be of aid to you, Lord Hosmer."

His smile was a little twisted.

"You are, Lady Charity, as loath as I am to admit it," he replied, making her smile back at him – albeit a little tentatively. "Now, I believe Lady Hayward is beckoning you towards her. I have evidently kept you here too long."

Charity glanced towards her chaperone and saw the

gentle expression on the lady's face, as well as the way that she tilted her head just a little, in order to pull Charity back towards her.

"You did not keep me here, Lord Hosmer," she answered, stepping back from him and bobbing a quick curtsey. "I chose to come and speak to you."

"Then I am grateful to you for your company and your willingness, Lady Charity," came the reply. "Thank you. I have something more to consider, I think."

She smiled at him and then turned away without a word. But when she glanced over her shoulder at him, she saw that Lord Hosmer was standing a little closer to the window, gazing out at the snow.

CHAPTER EIGHT

As much as Benedict did not want to admit it, much of what Lady Charity had said to him last evening made sense. He had found himself considering what she had said for many hours, to the point that he had returned home from the soiree and been entirely unable to retire to bed. Instead, he had sat in front of the fire in his study and, with a glass of whisky in his hand, had considered many things carefully.

Lady Charity had told him that, if his mind was filled with memories which made him blue-devilled, then instead of allowing them to come to him heedlessly, allowing them to fill him entirely, he ought to attempt to find something better with which to replace such thoughts.

Benedict grimaced as he sat back in his chair, finding himself still thinking about Lady Charity, even though it was now the following afternoon. The snow had become a little more relentless, falling all through the night so that there was now a blanket of white everywhere. Rising from his chair, Benedict made his way to the window and looked out, trying to suppress the dark memories which came flooding back.

Sighing heavily, he ran one hand across his forehead and tried to push them away, but still they continued to plague him. Lady Frederica had not permitted him to join her in the drawing room but, rather, had come to stand at the front door of the townhouse whilst he stood, confused and uncertain, in the snow outside.

It was then she had told him that she was no longer interested in their courtship. Their engagement, which had taken place only a day or so before, and had thankfully not been announced to the world yet, was now at an end. There was nothing between them any longer.

Benedict had not understood. Having been filled with such great happiness, such overwhelming joy, he had found himself crashing into despondency and sorrow as Lady Frederica had told him that there was to be no longer any connection between them. He had stood there in the snow, seeing the flakes falling between them and tried desperately to understand all that she had meant. Of course, it had taken a few days for him to realize that she truly was no longer eager to be courted by him but had, instead, decided to accept the attentions of another – one who had a little more wealth and a little more property than he.

And he had thought that she held a deep affection for him! The thought was practically laughable now, for she had never said such words to him and had never expressed any emotions akin to that. He had merely assumed that simply because *he* felt that way, she did also.

How wrong he had been.

"But I do not need to continually remember her now," he told himself aloud, recalling what Lady Charity had said. "To find something new, something beautiful and pleasing will aid me in forgetting such dark times."

Tilting his head, Benedict closed his eyes and tried to think on what he might consider instead.

In an instant, Lady Charity came to mind. The way she had looked up into his face last evening, the determination in her gaze and the slight lift of her chin that had told him she was not about to give up in the face of his anger all came back to him in an instant. The snow had been falling outside then and he had felt his heart soften at the expression on her face as she had watched it. It had been clear that she found a great joy and delight in watching the snow fall and he had found himself momentarily transfixed, taking her in and seeing the smile that spread so lightly across her face.

She was quite lovely, was she not?

Benedict sighed and opened his eyes. Yes, Lady Charity had been quite lovely in that moment and, were he honest with himself, he would have to state that he considered her to be more than a little beautiful. And yet it was the determination she had to remain dedicated to her cause in the face of his obvious irritation and upset, which impressed him most. A tirade of questions about why he had been so despondent had not followed the revelation he had given her about the reasons for his melancholy and, despite his frustration and clear dislike of their conversation, she had spoken to him with kindness, her sweet nature revealed to him once more. He had not told her that Lady Frederica's mother, Lady Dewsbury, had joined the soiree – something he had not at all expected. Nor had he stated the many sharp and painful emotions that had poured into his heart as he had watched the lady, remembering the times he had shared with Lady Frederica all over again.

Benedict shook his head to himself and ran one hand over his eyes. He did not want to think of the lady, did not want to have to feel the very same pain over and over again. Perhaps he would have to recall Lady Charity instead of Lady Frederica whenever he looked out at the falling snow.

"My Lord?"

Benedict turned around to see his butler standing in the doorway, an apologetic expression on his face.

"I do not think you heard my knock, Lord Hosmer," the butler continued, coming closer as Benedict beckoned him in. "You have a letter."

"Thank you," Benedict replied, not at all irritated by his servant's actions. "I was deep in thought."

He took the letter from the butler and then dismissed him, stating that, should he need to reply, he would simply ring the bell. The butler left the room and Benedict opened the letter at once, snapping the wax seal in half as he did so.

"'Lord Hosmer'," he read aloud, his brows furrowing. "'I do hope that you are neither frustrated nor angry with me for the words I spoke last evening. On reflection, I fear that some of my words may have been a little brash and inconsiderate and for that, I can only apologize. I do hope that we might speak again very soon.'"

A small smile crept across Benedict's face as he read Lady Charity's letter. Obviously, she too had been doing a great deal of thinking and now feared that she had spoken out of turn in some way. The urge to inform her that it was not so and that he was more than contented with all that had passed between them began to grow quickly within his heart. Another glance out of the window told him that it was a little foolish to step outside but, with a small shrug, Benedict turned towards the door and made his way towards it. He would call upon Lady Charity and make certain that she knew there was no upset there. He wanted to reassure her, to thank her and, perhaps, to tell her that she had been quite correct in her suggestions. That he *would* find a way to remove these painful memories from the forefront of his mind. With a smile beginning to spread across his face, Benedict made his way back to his bedchamber and rang the bell for his valet.

HAVING DISCOVERED that the two ladies had chosen to brave the cold and made their way to Gunter's tea shop for a warming beverage, Benedict had chosen to follow after them, although he prayed that Gunter's would be very warm indeed given that, even in his boots, greatcoat and gloves, he still felt very chilled indeed! Given that Gunter's was usually known for its ices and sweet treats during the height of summer, it was a little unusual to step inside to find no such things on display. The tea shop was, however, rather cozy with only a small space for patrons but a good deal of warmth – much to Benedict's relief!

"My Lord."

A shop worker bowed and looked expectantly towards Benedict.

"I am here seeking Lady Hayward and Lady Charity," Benedict told him. "Have they arrived?"

"Indeed, my Lord."

The man showed him quickly to a small table at the very back of the premises and Benedict felt a little gratified when he saw the surprise leap into Lady Charity's eyes.

"Lady Charity, Lady Hayward," he said, bowing low before them as they both began to rise. "Pray, stay seated. I came to call upon you, only to learn that you had braved the cold to venture here!"

Lady Hayward laughed and gestured for him to come and sit with them.

"Indeed we did, Lord Hosmer," she said, as Lady Charity watched him closely, no smile on her face. "It may have been a little foolish, given the amount of snow that has fallen but we were quite determined to venture out!"

"Then I applaud you," he replied, with a small inclination of his head. "You do not mind if I join you for a short time?"

"Of course we do not," Lady Hayward replied, as Lady Charity shook her head and attempted to smile, even though there was still a startled look in her eyes. "Please. Shall we order more tea?"

"Lady Hayward?"

Benedict looked over his shoulder to see Lady Riverland standing just behind him, a bright smile on her face.

"Good afternoon!" Lady Hayward cried, quickly rising from her chair. "I did not expect to see you here! Were you as brave as we?"

Turning back to Lady Charity as the two older ladies continued to speak, Benedict gave her what he hoped was a warm smile.

"I received your letter, Lady Charity," he said, quietly. "I wanted to call upon you at once, to make certain that you were fully aware that there is no upset nor frustration on my part. I feel nothing but contentment as regards our conversation last evening, Lady Charity."

Her eyes were still wide but, as he continued to smile at her, Benedict saw how a dusky pink began to enter her cheeks.

"I am relieved to hear you say so, Lord Hosmer," she replied, after a moment or two. "I began to be anxious that I had been much too forward or inconsiderate."

"You were neither," he replied, only to see the shop waiter come towards him, clearly ready to see what it was Benedict wished to order.

"Should you wish for something more, Lady Charity?" he asked, and was glad when she decided that she would like a little more tea. Seeing that Lady Hayward and Lady Riverland had sat down at an adjacent table, clearly quite contented to leave Benedict and Lady

Charity to converse together, Benedict quickly made his order and then returned to their conversation.

"I have considered all that you have said, Lady Charity," he continued, as the blush in her cheeks mounted just a little. "You are, I believe, quite correct." He grimaced, although his smile quickly returned to his face. "I should not like Lord and Lady Ramsbury to hear such a thing from me, however. You shall have to promise not to say a word to them!"

This, much to his relief, made Lady Charity laugh, her eyes brightening and no longer holding that sense of shock which had been there at the first.

"I have found being in London at Christmas time to be very difficult indeed," he continued, now speaking with a little more seriousness. "But I have found it all the worse to remain at my estate, entirely alone! I did try to do so one Christmas season but found myself so despondent that I made my way to London despite the treacherous weather!" Shaking his head at the memory, Benedict saw the concern in Lady Charity's eyes and felt his heart soften. "It is a very odd situation, I am aware, but it is as though being in London reminds me of what occurred whilst, at the same time, lifting my spirits just enough so that I might endure the trial without too much of a struggle."

"Whatever occurred has clearly had a very grave impact upon you, Lord Hosmer," she replied, keeping her voice low and quiet. "But if I have been able to encourage you in any way thus far, then I am very glad indeed."

A sudden urge to tell Lady Charity the truth about what had happened filled Benedict completely. He had not spoken of it at length to anyone for some time, had kept the pain of it wrapped up around his heart and yet, now that he looked into Lady Charity's eyes, knowing full well that she was truly eager to be of aid to him, that desire began to burn all through him.

"I was betrothed," he found himself saying, just as the shop waiter brought their tea, along with the small selection of cakes which Benedict had ordered. He waited until the waiter had set down their items and stepped away before continuing, nodding when Lady Charity offered to pour their tea.

"The lady in question was someone I considered to honest, trustworthy and true," he continued, unable to look Lady Charity in the face, but instead watching as the tea ran into the china cup. "I came to care for her a great deal. We were – we were just betrothed."

Lady Charity set down the teapot carefully.

"I see," she said, gently. "But that betrothal came to an end, I presume?"

Benedict felt his shoulders slump.

"It did," he told her, shaking his head. "But it was not my doing. Lady Frederica – for that was her name – decided that our betrothal was not something she wanted to continue – yet three days before, she had accepted when I asked her. I am only grateful that it had not been widely announced at that point, or my mortification would have been extreme, and her reputation damaged by her actions. She told me this as I stood on the steps outside her father's townhouse, when the snow was falling heavily. I could even hear the sound of someone playing the pianoforte and singing with such great gusto that it was as though they were attempting to serenade my deep distress." Swallowing hard as another stab of pain lanced his heart, Benedict continued on quietly. "It appeared that what I believed to be within her heart was not, in fact, present. I later learned that the Marquess of Norwich had shown an interest in Lady Frederica – and thus, she had chosen to accept his court rather than continue with our betrothal." A rueful smile pulled at his lips. "It seems that a Marquess with a greater fortune than I was the better prospect. I was thoroughly rejected, Lady Charity."

The lady held his gaze steadily and, much to his surprise, he saw her eyes glistening. Was she truly sorry for him? Was that genuine compassion which filled her gaze? His heart lurched and he looked away, picking up his tea cup and taking a small sip in the hope that it would mask his true emotions.

"That must have been truly dreadful, Lord Hosmer."

Closing his eyes for a moment, Benedict nodded.

"It was," he agreed, his whole body beginning to feel a little weak, now that he had told her the truth of it all. "However, I confess that I felt nothing but foolishness, rather than anything else. I realized that I had given a good deal of my time and, indeed, my emotions to someone who was playing me for a fool. What I believed I saw in Lady Frederica was not truly there. Perhaps I only *wished* to see it."

"And you are reminded of it all when you return to London at Christmas time," Lady Charity said, clearly understanding. "Might I ask how long ago it was?"

"It was some years back," Benedict confessed.

"Which is why, Lady Charity, I have come to see that what you said to me about replacing my dark memories with ones that bring me a little more happiness is quite correct. I have been unwilling to do so. It is as though I am quite contented with how I feel and how I behave – which, even though I know I said as much to you, is not the truth. I do not want to remember her any longer. I do not want to remember the pain. There must be some sort of joy that I can have, that I can *find* which will, I hope, change what I feel at present."

"Oh, Lord Hosmer, of course there is!"

It took a moment for Benedict to realize that Lady Charity had placed her hand over his as it rested on the table, for he was so taken with the expression of eagerness on her face and the excitement in her voice that he could not look away from her. It was only when warmth began to spread through his fingers that he glanced down to see her hand on his and, much to his surprise, he felt a great sense of true contentment fill him.

"I should be glad to continue to aid you, in whatever way I can," Lady Charity continued, quickly removing her hand as her color rose. "There is such a delight to be had in this time of year and I can only pray that you will discover even a little of it, so that your Christmas will be more than a little joyful."

"That is very kind of you, Lady Charity, and I certainly have no unwillingness when it comes to accepting your offer," he replied, honestly. "I do not wish to be such a burden any longer. I do not wish to *carry* such a burden either!"

"Then I am certain that change will come about,"

Lady Charity replied, happily. "I am so very glad indeed that you came in to speak to me, Lord Hosmer. I confess I was rather anxious that I had overstepped after last evening's conversation."

Benedict shook his head.

"It was what I needed to hear," he said, quietly wondering why Ramsbury's advice – which had always been to forget entirely about Lady Frederica and focus on what was present – had never had such an effect upon him. "Thank you, Lady Charity."

The door to Gunter's opened and, just as Benedict was about to pick up his tea cup for another sip, a loud laugh startled him. A little irritated, he glanced over his shoulder at the incomers – only for everything within him to freeze at once.

He could not look away, his eyes fixed to the lady who had just entered the tea rooms. She was rubbing her gloved hands together and talking loudly to another – another that Benedict recognized. Why had he not known she was in London? She had never once returned to town since her marriage to the Lord Norwich, so why then was she here?

"Lord Hosmer?"

A gentle hand touched his and he swung back around rather sharply, catching Lady Charity by surprise.

"Forgive me," he said hastily, realizing just how close he'd come to knocking over the tea pot in his haste to turn back towards her. "I – I confess I am a little shocked, that is all."

Lady Charity's eyes widened.

"Indeed?"

He nodded, his heart beating painfully in his chest. All manner of emotions were flooding him now, from anger, to sorrow, to the urgent desire to escape.

"I – I believe that Lady Frederica – I mean, that is to say, Lady Norwich – has returned to London," he said, seeing Lady Charity's eyes flare with astonishment. "And that she has just now stepped into Gunter's tea room, alongside her mother."

It took a moment for Lady Charity to respond.

"I see," she said, giving herself a slight shake and putting a smile on her lips which Benedict presumed was nothing more than practical. "That should not matter to you, Lord Hosmer. You are doing all you can to forget the situation, are you not? If she is returned to London, then what of it?"

Benedict shook his head, unable to sort one swirling emotion from the other.

"It is not as simple as you make out, Lady Charity," he replied, tersely. "You understand that I have not set eyes upon her since –"

"But what does that matter now?" she interrupted, picking up her tea cup and taking a sip before she continued. "If you allow yourself to become overwhelmed, then you are remaining precisely where you are at present. You remain the gentleman who cannot forget her, who cannot let go of his pain. Were you not telling me only a few minutes ago that this was not the sort of life you wished to lead any longer? That you were eager to remove yourself from it?"

The answer was there on his lips but Benedict could

not speak it. The room seemed to shrink around him, the air growing a little less as he curled one hand into a fist in an attempt to keep himself entirely composed.

"I – I must leave you."

He rose without warning, the cups and saucers rattling as he did so.

"Excuse me."

He was being both rude and foolish, he knew, but Benedict did not care. The only thing he wanted was to make his way out of the tearoom before Lady Norwich saw him. He needed time to think on this, time to consider what he might do, now that he knew she was returned. Everything in him screamed with either confusion or pain and, even though he wanted to look back at Lady Charity, wanted to behave with much more decorum, Benedict found that he simply could not do so. Keeping his head low and pulling his hat down a little more, Benedict pulled open the door and stepped outside into the cold air.

It was only then that he finally felt he could breathe again, his chest still tight and his heart pounding.

Lady Norwich was back in London. And it seemed that she was, once again, about to throw everything into confusion.

CHAPTER NINE

Walking in to dinner was one thing but being seated across from a lady who Charity knew all too well was the source of Lord Hosmer's consternation was quite another. Charity had been introduced to Lady Norwich and to her mother, Lady Dewsbury. She had been hard pressed to keep her expression calm and clear, knowing full well that the lady before her was the one who had broken Lord Hosmer's heart.

"You have done very well thus far, Lady Charity," Lady Hayward murmured, as they waited in preparation for the first of their courses to be served. "I can imagine that such an introduction must have been a little... interesting."

Charity gave her companion a quick, wry smile.

"Indeed it was," she agreed, softly. "But I shall not judge the lady. It is not my place to do so, given that *I* am not Lord Hosmer and I have only heard what he has said about the matter."

It went against her conscience to speak so but

Charity was quite determined that, despite her own thoughts and determinations, she would not be judgmental when it came to the lady. She was merely another acquaintance and, should Charity not have known anything about her, she was sure that she would have found Lady Norwich very pleasant indeed.

"I was very sorry to hear of your loss, Lady Norwich," said one of the guests, as the soup was set before them. "That must have been a very trying time for you."

Lady Norwich smiled back at the lady, although it was, Charity considered, something of a sad expression.

"Thank you," she said, quietly. "It is difficult to consider that it occurred a little over a year ago, for it feels like such a very long time since then."

"But of course it must," the same lady replied, kindly. "You must feel his loss very heavily indeed."

Charity cast a quick glance towards Lady Hayward who gave a small shake of her head at Charity's look. It was clear that neither of them knew precisely what Lady Norwich was speaking of but, given the time that she had spoken of, Charity began to wonder if Lord Norwich had been the one to pass away. That would make sense, given that Lady Norwich was present – and appeared to be residing – with her mother.

"His passing has not been made very well known," said another, speaking now to Lady Dewsbury. "Have you found it a trial to have to inform so many people?"

Lady Dewsbury sighed in a dramatic fashion, one hand going to her forehead for a moment.

"Lord Norwich was a very *private* gentleman," she said, her words spoken with a great sense of gravitas. "His passing was noted by his friends and family but, given the time of year and the difficulties with the roads..." She sighed heavily and shook her head. "It was, as you say, kept rather quiet."

"But I am back within society now, and have greatly enjoyed my first few days back in London," Lady Norwich replied, with what appeared to be a very brave smile. "It is a relief to be back amongst the *beau monde* and to find solace, comfort and companionship with my very dear friends."

She looked around the table as though each and every person present was one that she valued very highly indeed, even though Charity had only been introduced to her some minutes before! Her words, however, were met with a murmur of approval and Lady Norwich smiled all the more, before the conversation turned to other things.

Charity could not help but feel a great swell of sympathy for the lady, regardless of what Lord Hosmer had told her. To lose one's husband must be very difficult indeed and she could only feel compassion for her circumstances. Quietly, she wondered if Lord Hosmer himself knew of such a thing, deciding that he must not know of it, given that he had not even been aware of Lady Norwich's return to London. Would it be right for her to tell him of what she had learned? Or would it be best for him to discover it in his own time? Sighing inwardly to herself as the conversation went on around her, Charity recalled just how abruptly Lord Hosmer had left the tearoom when he had seen Lady Norwich again. The look on his face had been one of both shock and dread and she had swiftly realized just how much he was struggling to keep his composure. Any attempt to imagine his feelings had been much too difficult for her and Charity had found her advice to be quickly disregarded by him also. It was not that she felt any insult at such disregard, but rather only a deep frustration that she was not able to aid him in any way.

"Try not to think of it at this present moment," came a quiet voice to her left and, as Charity started violently, she realized that she had been lost in her own thoughts and, therefore, had not been paying any attention to the conversations going on around her. Casting a quick smile in Lady Hayward's direction, she forced herself to push all thought of Lord Hosmer to the back of her mind and to concentrate solely on behaving with all decorum and propriety for the rest of the evening.

~

"Good evening, Lord Ramsbury."

Charity curtsied quickly, seeing the broad smile settle on Lord Ramsbury's face as he greeted her. She hoped he had not noticed the way she had been searching the room with her gaze in the expectation of seeing Lord Hosmer! It had been some days since she had last been in his company and, whilst she would not permit herself to say that she missed him, there was certainly an eagerness in her heart to see him again. That came entirely from wanting to make certain that he was quite well, she told herself, given that he had left so abruptly when Lady Norwich had first been seen. On top of that, she also had decided to inform him of Lady Norwich's loss, rather than permit him to discover such a thing himself. The only problem as yet was that she had not seen hide nor hair of him these last few days!

"Good evening, Lady Charity, Lady Hayward," Lord Ramsbury replied, just as his wife came to join him. "I had hoped you would be here this evening!"

"Oh?" Charity replied, smiling quickly at Lady Ramsbury who returned her smile with one of her own. "Is there some particular reason for such a hope, Lord Ramsbury?"

Lord and Lady Ramsbury exchanged glances, only for Lord Ramsbury's smile to fade somewhat. Charity's heart began to quicken its pace as she took in the looks and felt herself begin to grow anxious.

"I had hoped to ask you, Lady Charity, whether or not you had been in the company of Lord Hosmer of late."

Charity frowned, her concern beginning to grow.

"It has been a few days since I was last in his company," she replied, honestly. "He joined us at Gunter's tearoom but since then, I have not seen him." She bit her lip, seeing how Lord and Lady Ramsbury glanced at each other again. "I – I should also mention that he left my company very quickly indeed, thanks to the sudden return of Lady Frederica? Or the widowed Lady Norwich, as she is now."

Lord Ramsbury let out a startled exclamation at this, his eyes wide as he stared at her.

"You – you are quite sure?" Lady Ramsbury asked, now speaking rather quickly. "You are certain of such a thing?"

Lady Hayward nodded and spoke before Charity could.

"Indeed. We were in her company only two days ago, at a dinner party. I had not met the lady before and as such, both myself and Lady Charity gained an introduction. We did not realize that she was widowed, however, until later on that evening."

Lord Ramsbury blew out a long breath, shaking his head as he did so and passing one hand over his eyes.

"I did not think she would return to London," he said, dropping his hand and looking towards his wife. "Lord Norwich was not the sort of gentleman who was eager to spend his time in society. I believe he was only in London that one Season to procure a bride. But to know now that he is gone and that she remains..."

He shook his head again and did not finish his sentence, leaving Lady Ramsbury to speak to Charity.

"And you say that Lord Hosmer is aware of her presence in London now?" she asked, as Charity nodded. "I am sorry if he was at all rude to you, but you must understand just how severely he feels with regard to her."

"I quite understand," Charity replied, firmly. "I have heard it all from him, although I have determined that I shall not judge the lady in question simply because of what I have been told. In truth, I feel a good deal of compassion for her, given that she has lost her husband at such a young age."

Lady Ramsbury held Charity's gaze for a few moments before she sighed and nodded, causing Charity to wonder if this meant that Lady Ramsbury approved of such considerations.

"You do not know the lady, of course, so it is wise for you to behave so," Lady Ramsbury said quietly, as Lord Ramsbury nodded his agreement. "But now I am concerned for Lord Hosmer. He has spent the last three years lost in grief, pain and despondency and, to see the lady in question again must, I am sure, only add to his feelings at present."

Charity hesitated before she spoke, not wishing to contradict Lady Ramsbury but being quite certain that what she had said of Lord Hosmer was a little mistaken.

"I – I believe that Lord Hosmer wished very much to no longer remain in such a state," she said, glancing towards Lady Hayward who smiled encouragingly. "He spoke of how he had been choosing to linger in such a frame of mind and how he no longer wished to do so. He stated, quite plainly, that it had been nothing more than a choice on his part to remain in melancholy, to allow himself to be reminded of what had occurred rather than encouraging himself to discover happier times that might push away the past." Her eyes drifted away as she smiled ruefully, her gaze now roving about the room instead of looking towards Lord and Lady Ramsbury. "He said as much just before Lady Norwich arrived," she finished, recalling just how much Lord Hosmer's demeanor had altered the moment he had set eyes on Lady Norwich again.

There was, within that memory, a small swell of pain that he had behaved in such a way, that he had been so quick to brush her aside and to escape from the tearoom, and now, Charity had to admit that such pain had only begun to grow with every day that she had neither seen nor heard from him. They had only just begun their acquaintance and he had only just agreed to accept her help when it came to the matter of his memories and his past, only for him to then recoil away from her the moment Lady Norwich had returned.

"That is very interesting," Lord Ramsbury murmured, as Charity turned her attention back to him and caught the sharp glint in his eyes. "I am glad that he was willing to do such a thing, Lady Charity, for I confess that both I and my dear wife have been saying much the same for many months and he has never once listened to us!"

Lady Ramsbury's smile was warm.

"You have reached him when we could not," she said, her hand out to rest on Charity's arm for a moment. "That was very well done, my dear friend."

Charity shook her head. "It counts for nothing if he is now keeping away from society because of Lady Norwich's presence," she said, a trifle glumly. "And I am not certain either that he is at all aware of her current situation."

"You mean to say that he does not know she is widowed," Lord Ramsbury clarified, as Charity nodded. "Well, that can be easily rectified. I –"

"Ramsbury!"

Charity could not help but turn her head and look behind her at the loud voice which had captured the attention of half the room. Much to her shock, Lord Hosmer appeared, a jaunty smile on his face as he came towards them.

"And Lady Charity!" he exclaimed, one hand

pressing her arm for a moment before he forced himself between Charity and Lady Ramsbury in order to stand next to Lord Ramsbury. "What excellent company we have!"

A little embarrassed and praying that none of the other guests would look across at them and pay Lord Hosmer too much attention, Charity lowered her gaze to the floor as a flush of heat crossed her face.

"Hosmer," Lord Ramsbury murmured, looking at his friend with a sharp eye. "We have not seen you in some days."

Lord Hosmer swayed slightly, one hand clutching a glass of brandy which sloshed dangerously near to the rim of his glass as he lifted his arm in gesticulation.

"That is because I have remained at home," he said, as Charity looked back at him carefully, taking in his flushed cheeks, the brightness to his eyes and the easy manner which had never been a part of his character before. "Did you know that *she* is returned to London?"

Charity's heart sank. It was clear that Lord Hosmer had been very badly affected by Lady Norwich's return to London. All that she had hoped for him, all that she had permitted herself to now expect, was gone in an instant.

"Ladies and gentlemen, we are now to make our way to the music room where we shall sing some carols together and listen to a few of the young ladies perform pieces for us also!"

The cry of their host brought Charity a little relief as she made to turn away, no longer wanting to be in Lord Hosmer's company. Her heart was aching terribly, disappointment and disillusionment filling her very marrow. It seemed that, regardless of what she had said to him, what she had encouraged him to think and to consider, he was going to be quite lost in his dark and desperate emotions when it came to Lady Norwich. Nothing she could say or do would help him. She had been foolish to even attempt to do so.

"Where are you going?"

Lord Hosmer's hand caught her arm and Charity was caught off guard, being pulled back in a none too gentle manner as she looked back at Lord Hosmer. His eyes were fixed to hers, his brow furrowed as he studied her features.

"Lord Hosmer, do release Lady Charity," Lady Hayward said, in a firm voice. "If you wish to join us, then do please attend us to the music room."

Lord Hosmer's jaw worked for a moment but, eventually, he let go of her arm and sighed heavily, dropping his head as he did so.

"I do not wish to sing carols," he stated, his shoulders slumping as all exuberance left him. "There is –"

A sense of anger began to burn in Charity and she took a small step towards him, cutting him off with her own hard words.

"There is no joy to be had, Lord Hosmer?" she asked, her voice a harsh whisper, although each word seemed to strike him hard, given how much he recoiled. "You find it much too painful to sing such words, since they will remind you of Lady Norwich? Therefore, you shun it entirely instead of choosing to do so in the hopes of pushing aside your difficult memories and discovering happier times? Yes, I am certain that you shall do so, for that is what you have been doing these last few years and now, it seems, you have every desire to continue to behave in such a way, regardless of what alternatives lie before you." She lifted her chin and glared at him, aware of the anger in her heart and allowing it to burn fiercely rather than make any attempt to dampen it. "Good evening, Lord Hosmer. I find that I no longer wish to be in your company."

Turning on her heel, she made her way to where Lady Hayward stood only a few steps away and, taking her chaperone's arm, walked with her into the music room. It took a great deal of effort to put a calm expression on her face and to hide the truth of what she felt but, with Lady Hayward guiding her, Charity soon found herself sitting down in a quiet corner of the room as the other guests continued to make their way into the room.

"You spoke sharply to Lord Hosmer." Charity nodded, glancing at Lady Hayward and fully expecting to see a gentle rebuke in her eyes but, much to her surprise, discovering that there was nothing of the sort present. "He has angered you?"

A sigh escaped from Charity's lips.

"I – I feel anger, yes," she admitted quietly, so that no-one else would overhear her. "To see him in such a state when he was so willing to do what he could to pull himself from this dark place has quite ruined my hope in him. I believed him when he stated that wanted very much to do as I had suggested."

"To find happiness in the season and all the joy that it can bring," Lady Hayward clarified, as Charity nodded.

"To choose not to dwell on the past hurts that once were present here."

"Indeed, that is it precisely," Charity replied, feeling that faint stirring of anger in her heart again. "But now to see him so makes me realize that there is no question of his doing so. It appears that Lady Norwich has the same hold on him as before. He has made not even a single attempt to free himself from all that he feels and remembers! Instead, he has chosen to hide himself away and, when he does return to society, to drink as much liquor as he requires in order to forget."

Lady Hayward held Charity's gaze for a long moment and then spread her hands.

"I wish I could find something of encouragement to say to you, my dear," she said, her expression one of great sympathy, "but all I can say at present is that I quite understand your feelings at this present moment. I too was rather... disappointed with his appearance this evening." After a moment of silence, she leaned forward and looked Charity directly in the eye. "But do not give up all hope," she finished, as Charity shook her head, unable to find even a modicum of such an emotion. "It may be that your words this evening will bring him back to where he was when he spoke to you in Gunter's."

"Or it may be that he will remove himself entirely from my company and decide to remain precisely as he is at present," Charity replied, darkly. "Perhaps I have been foolish, Lady Hayward. I have been so busy considering Lord Hosmer that I have not once permitted myself to consider other gentlemen who might be of greater benefit to me in their company than he."

Something flickered in Lady Hayward's eyes.

"Or it may be that you have found someone who has caught your attention in a way that no other has as yet," she said, just as their host rose from his chair, ready to announce the first song they might sing together. "Consider all that you feel, Lady Charity, and realize that Lord Hosmer might be slowly becoming more to you than you have ever expected."

CHAPTER TEN

I t was not entirely unexpected for Benedict to awaken with such a great pain in his head that it took all the willpower he had to simply lift his head from his pillow. He had spent the last few days doing very little other than wandering about his townhouse, a glass in his hand and a great many thoughts pounding into his mind, one after the other.

Although, he considered, groaning loudly as he sat up, perhaps it had been very foolish indeed to go into society when he was not quite prepared for such a thing. What if he had seen Lady Norwich? What if she had been present at the little soiree? Then what would he have done?

Closing his eyes, Benedict let out another groan and reached to ring the bell, choosing to spend the remainder of the day in much the same way as he had the morning. It was, no doubt, already luncheon and Benedict had no desire whatsoever to go anywhere other than perhaps his study for a short time. Somewhere, in the back of his mind, he recalled that he had accepted an invitation to a ball or some such thing that evening, but given that it would be busy with guests, Benedict did not think that anyone would miss him should he not attend.

"My Lord?"

Benedict opened his eyes and looked into the face of the footman who now stood just inside the door. It took a few minutes for the man's face to come into focus, and Benedict, when he spoke, felt as though his throat was filled with pieces of sharp stone which grated horribly with every word.

"Have coffee sent up," he said, wanting nothing other than to lie back down again. "At once."

The footman inclined his head.

"Yes, my Lord. And, if I might be so bold as to ask, when do you think you will be rising?"

Benedict frowned.

"I do not know," he said, rigidly. "Now, the coffee."

Again, the footman hesitated and Benedict felt a sharp edge of anger begin to stab at his heart. He was about to speak out again, to demand that the fellow do as was asked of him, else be in fear for his position at Benedict's home, only for the footman to speak again.

"It is only that Lord Ramsbury is waiting to have an audience with you, my Lord," he said, sending Benedict's anger spiraling away. "He insisted that we did not wake you but has chosen to remain here waiting."

The pain in Benedict's head seemed to redouble as he looked back at the footman, who was now shifting from foot to foot, evidently aware that he had upset Benedict a little by such an explanation.

"And how long has he been waiting?" Benedict found himself asking, even though he wanted nothing more than to tell the footman to order Ramsbury from the house. It was only knowledge of Ramsbury's determination that kept him from saying so, for his friend would not be deterred by a simple request from Benedict. "And what time is it?"

"It is gone three in the afternoon, my Lord," the footman replied, making Benedict start with surprise. "Lord Ramsbury has been here some two hours, I believe."

A sense of shame began to creep over Benedict as he groaned and dropped his head into his hands. He did not speak for some moments but, eventually, let out a long sigh.

"Have the coffee brought still, but send for my valet," he bit out, wishing that Ramsbury had chosen to spend the afternoon elsewhere. "I will be down momentarily. And make certain that Lord Ramsbury has all that he requires until I arrive."

The footman nodded, a flash of relief covering his expression for a moment before, after a final enquiry as to whether there was anything else that Benedict needed, he exited the room and left Benedict alone.

Benedict sighed heavily and rubbed at his forehead, wishing that the pain would dissipate just a little. He had been thinking that a quiet afternoon was all that he needed, all that he wanted, only for it now to be stolen from him. With another pained sigh, he swung himself out of bed and forced himself to the chair by the fireplace, glad that the maids had made certain to have his room warm and ready for him when the time came for him to rise. The wood crackled as it burned and Benedict looked glumly into the flames, finding himself rather filled with despondency at the thought of having to go and speak to Ramsbury.

"Most likely he will berate me for last evening," Benedict muttered to himself, suddenly recalling just how much he had drunk and having a vague memory of speaking with Lord and Lady Ramsbury.

He had not joined the other guests when they had gone to sing carols together, but had decisively made his way from the townhouse, having chosen to take his leave rather than remain and join in with such festivities. That would only remind him of what Lady Frederica had done and that, coupled with the awareness that she was now in London, made things all the worse.

"Your coffee, my Lord."

Benedict reached out and took the cup at once, seeing the footman standing respectfully to one side.

"Pray, go and make certain that Lord Ramsbury does not lack refreshments," he said, as the coffee began to warm him through, sending a fresh heat into his very bones. "And inform him that I shall join him within the hour."

The footman nodded and quit the room without a word, closing the door tightly behind him. Benedict grimaced and picked up his cup once more, taking another sip before setting it back down again. There was a tartness to the coffee which seemed to awaken him a little more, seemed to take some of the pain from his head, and yet Benedict knew that he would have to be a good deal more himself before he could face Ramsbury. The last thing he needed was to attempt to speak to his friend when there was nothing but confusion and pain coming from both his head and his heart! Ramsbury would just have to wait a little longer.

≈

"WHATEVER WERE YOU THINKING?"

Benedict winced as a fresh wave of pain sliced through his head.

"You need not raise your voice so, Ramsbury," he muttered, walking across the room and throwing himself into a chair near the fire. "Surely you must be aware of the state I am in at present?"

Ramsbury's eyes narrowed.

"I care nothing for how you feel," he stated, angrily. "To behave with such a lack of decorum and consideration is both ridiculous and inconsiderate. Have you any idea of just how upset Lady Charity was at your behavior?"

"I – I recall very little," Benedict replied, truthfully. "Although, now that I think on it...." He trailed off, his brow furrowing as he looked away from his friend, suddenly remembering a very distressed and angry Lady Charity as she had stood before him, words flinging themselves from her mouth. "She – she was angry with me, was she not?"

"And rightly so!" Ramsbury retorted, furiously. "You were foxed and half-witted last evening, Hosmer! And all because a lady from three years past has decided to return to London! I may not have called you a fool before, but I shall do so now!" Wincing, but refusing to say anything which would justify him to Ramsbury – for, indeed, there was nothing for him to say – Benedict put his head in his hands and let out a long, heavy sigh. "Just because Lady Norwich has come back to London does not mean that you should throw aside all that you have only *just* begun to discover," Ramsbury continued, clearly still very angry. "You stated to Lady Charity that you realized the merit of what she had suggested, told her that you would be glad of her aid, only to then behave in a manner which told Lady Charity that you have no real intention of doing so. You saw Lady Norwich again, left Lady Charity in great haste and, since then, have done nothing but mope around in your townhouse until you decided to attend a soiree and drink more than you ought. In addition, you then made such a fool of yourself that even Lady Charity spoke out against your behavior – and, as I have said, with every right to her vehemence in doing so. And what is worse, the fact that you cannot see what is right before your face makes you all the more ridiculous. I am ashamed to call you my friend at this present moment, Hosmer. Something must be done."

Benedict lifted his head from his hands. He had never seen Ramsbury in such a state of anger before, had never heard him speak with such force! The words jarred him, made him question all that he had been doing and forced him to look again at his own behavior.

"I – I am sorry." Ramsbury's brows lifted in evident surprise, perhaps having expected Benedict to do nothing other than defend his actions. "You must understand that seeing Lady Frederica – that is, Lady Norwich – again came as a great shock."

Ramsbury threw up his hands.

"But why should it be so?" he demanded, his eyes wide with evident frustration at Benedict's ridiculous words. "It has been three years! I know you cared for her, but surely what she chose to do made you realize her true nature! You cannot surely consider yourself to still care for her in that same way?"

"Indeed, I do not!" Benedict exclaimed, almost appalled at the idea. "But when I saw her, the very same –"

"You recalled all that had occurred and it brought you a great deal of pain," Ramsbury said, wearily, shaking his head. "Yes, Hosmer. I have heard you say similar things before. That is why you find no enjoyment in all that this wonderful time of year can bring. You are *choosing* to remain there, choosing to remain in the shadows rather than step out into the light. And, in doing so, you are missing all that is before you, all that could be if only you would grasp it." He dropped his hands and closed his eyes, his voice no longer as loud as it had been. "And it will escape from you before you realize."

Benedict frowned, looking steadily at his friend and trying to make sense of what he said.

"What will escape from me?" he asked, as Ramsbury sighed heavily and threw him a weary look. "What is it that I am missing?"

Ramsbury said nothing, looking back at Benedict steadily for some minutes before he muttered something Benedict could not hear, and clasped his hands tightly behind his back, turning his head away. Benedict had the distinct impression that he was the sole cause of Ramsbury's great frustration and that, he had to admit, made him rather embarrassed.

"Lady Charity is before you," Ramsbury stated, astonishing Benedict. "Do you truly believe that her only interest in you is gratitude for what you did with Lord Amundsen?" He laughed, the sound brittle and harsh. "It may have been so at the first but I can assure you that it is now not the only reason for her interest in you."

Benedict shook his head, a tightness in his chest that had not been there before.

"That is nonsense," he said, determinedly. "Lady Charity is nothing more than a kind-hearted creature who has sought to aid this poor fool towards a happier path. And she has done so *solely* to repay me for my actions with Lord Amundsen – which, I recall informing her, was not at all necessary."

"You may believe that, but both my good wife and I think you are quite mistaken," Ramsbury replied, firmly. "Lady Charity is all that you have described, however. She has a good nature, is very generous indeed and has a kindness about her that is evident to all. But that kindness and generosity of spirit has been pushed or directed to you. And to you alone, Hosmer."

Benedict wanted to scoff at this, wanted to state that his friend was quite mistaken, but there came a sudden heat that ran from his head to the very soles of his feet as he thought about what Ramsbury had said.

"You mean to suggest that there is an opportunity for a further acquaintance between myself and Lady Charity?" Benedict asked, as Ramsbury nodded. "I – I cannot think so. I –"

"As I have said, you have been so caught up with Lady Norwich that you have not seen what is right before your eyes," Ramsbury interrupted, finally calm enough to sit down and look directly at Benedict without anger burning in his eyes. "I should not like to suggest that Lady Charity is simply waiting for you to notice her, however. Although I believe that your acquaintance can, in time, bring about a great happiness for you both, should you be willing to pursue it."

Benedict did not know what to say, feeling himself quite overwhelmed by such a statement, and yet realizing that what Ramsbury was saying about his lack of awareness and his tendency to become entirely caught up with Lady Norwich was, of course, quite correct. As for Lady Charity, however, he had not even *thought* about such a thing and, therefore, could not yet properly consider what he felt about the idea.

"Forget Lady Norwich," Ramsbury said, quietly. "Forget what she chose, forget the pain and choose to leave it in the past where it belongs. For too long, you have dwelt on the pain that this time of year brings to you rather than considering what might be waiting for you here, should you only look. I have done what I can to encourage you out of such a situation but it has been Lady Charity who has finally managed to do so." One shoulder lifted. "I think that speaks for itself, does it not?"

Benedict was not quite sure what to say to such a remark, looking at his friend and feeling both embarrassment and shame creep over his heart.

"What must I do?" he said eventually, as Ramsbury lifted one eyebrow. "Lady Charity, you said, was very upset last evening. There must be something I can do or say that will, in some small way, make recompense?

Ramsbury looked away, his brow furrowing and his lips twisted and pulled to one side as he considered.

"I suppose," he said, slowly, "that you will have to find a way to prove to Lady Charity that you are *not* as caught up with Lady Norwich's return as she believes you to be. She needs to see that you are making every attempt to step away from your past memories and look now to the future. When you see Lady Norwich again – as you are certain to do given that she is now in society – you must be cordial but nothing more. Be entirely unaffected."

"I – I am not certain that I can be," Benedict replied, a little gruffly. "It is easy enough to say but –"

"Prepare yourself, if you must," Ramsbury interrupted, his tone now rather practical. "And whatever you feel, do not permit it to permeate your behavior nor your manner. Consider what and who you have before you, *particularly* if it is Lady Charity."

Letting out a small sigh, Benedict let his resolve begin to grow steadily.

"Very well," he said, as Ramsbury nodded, a somewhat contented expression settling across his face. "I shall try, of course."

The thought of seeing Lady Norwich again, of being in her company and having to greet her as though nothing whatsoever had occurred between them, was one that wrapped itself tightly around Benedict's heart and squeezed hard. However, the thought of having to speak to Lady Charity again, to apologize and to attempt to make amends, now realizing what might be between them, should he pursue it, made his considerations all the more fierce.

"I am glad to hear it," Ramsbury replied. "Now, you are to attend Lord Whitegates's ball this evening, are you not? I am certain that both Lady Charity *and* Lady Norwich will be present."

Benedict found himself nodding, even though he had already decided to remain at home for the rest of the day and night.

"I will attend, of course," he said, evidently willing to resign himself to the fact that he would now be going regardless of what he had thought previously. "And mayhap spend the little time I have left before then to consider all that you have said."

Ramsbury nodded.

"Very good, Hosmer," he replied, now a good deal calmer than before. "And let us hope that this night, you will not be as eager to imbibe as much brandy as before!"

"I certainly shall not do so," Benedict replied, ruefully. "Of that, Ramsbury, I am quite determined."

STEPPING into Lord Whitegate's ball filled Benedict with more nervousness than he had experienced in some time. Just knowing that both Lady Charity and Lady Norwich were present filled him with such anxiety that he felt like turning around and making his way directly back to his carriage. But no, he was not about to show such cowardice. He had behaved foolishly and it was right for him to make amends as best he could with Lady Charity, and he had spent the afternoon considering what he might say to Lady Norwich, should he meet her again. No longer was he filled with that same ire, the same lingering pain which had caught him so many times before. There was, of course, the urge to press his mind back to that moment, to see the greenery decorating the ballroom and to let himself recall the happy times he had spent with Lady Norwich *before* she had brought their betrothal to an end – but Benedict was determined not to do so. He had lived too long in such memories and now, if he was to find any happiness at all, he needed to be determined in his efforts.

Walking through the ballroom, he smiled and nodded at various guests before, finally, he caught sight of his quarry. Lady Charity was standing with Lady Hayward and talking with another young lady and someone Benedict presumed was the young lady's mother. There was a warm smile on Lady Charity's lips and none of the anger that he had managed to recall from last evening.

If only she would look at me in such a way.

The thought came unbidden to his mind as he stood still, looking at the lady and finding his heart quickening in a manner that astonished him greatly. Had Ramsbury been correct? Had he simply not *seen* her in this particular way before?

Her eyes flicked towards him for just a moment, as though she knew that he was watching her, and Benedict quickly darted his own gaze away, although it was much too late. Embarrassment brought a fresh warmth to his face but he remained precisely where he was, uncertain whether or not to approach Lady Charity.

"Good evening, Lord Hosmer. I did wonder when we might see each other again."

A familiar voice reached his ears and the warmth he felt was chased away in an instant as he turned to his left. Lady Norwich was standing there, entirely unaccompanied, it seemed, her eyes searching his face with evidently eager expectation – although quite what she was hoping for, Benedict could not say.

He cleared his throat and looked back at her steadily.

"Good evening, Lady Norwich," he said, taking in her familiar features but, to his surprise, feeling no hint of longing, no sudden swell of pain. He found himself rather detached, in fact, perhaps all too aware of Lady Charity nearby. "I did not know you had returned to London."

"I have indeed," she answered, her eyes bright and a small smile on her face, as though she was attempting to prove just how glad she was to see him again, although Benedict suspected that she was also hiding the truth of her emotions from him. "I thought to spend Christmas in London this year, in an attempt to make my situation a little happier." She looked away for a moment, her smile fading. "It would be better than remaining at my small estate alone, certainly."

Benedict, slightly uncertain as to what the lady meant, said nothing but found himself clearing his throat again, turning his head away for a moment or two.

"And you are quite contented, Lord Hosmer?" Lady Norwich asked. "You are not wed, as yet?"

A little taken aback by the question, Benedict looked at her sharply but there was nothing but a gentle interest on the lady's face.

"No," he replied, tightly. "I am not yet wed."

"Well, I am certain that whichever lady you choose will be very contented with the match indeed," she replied, confusing him all the more. If he was correct, there was a small hint of regret in her voice but, then again, he might only be hearing what he wished to hear. Part of him, certainly, wanted her to feel regret and shame for what she had done, but Benedict knew that to be eager for such a thing was foolishness indeed.

"Are you inclined to dance this evening?" she asked him but Benedict quickly shook his head. Nothing could interest him less than taking Lady Norwich in his arms and stepping out with her, and he wanted to make such a thing very clear indeed.

"I do not find myself inclined to dancing," he stated, a little coldly. "You must understand, Lady Norwich. There is a good deal about this time of year that lacks the enjoyment it once had."

He had not meant to say such a thing, had not meant to fill his words with the sound of accusation but yet they had escaped from him and, as he looked into her face, Benedict saw that she understood precisely what he meant.

"I see," came the quiet reply, her smile no longer present. "I quite understand, Lord Hosmer. I confess that

I am not particularly eager to dance either, given that I am still wrapped up in sorrow."

Benedict frowned.

"Sorrow?" he repeated, as Lady Norwich nodded. "I – I am sorry to hear that, Lady Norwich."

"Are you indeed?" Her voice had become a little sharper, her eyes now a trifle narrowed. "I had thought that you might be a little glad to hear of my suffering, Lord Hosmer." Her suggestion brought a stab of guilt to his heart for, even though he was quite unsure as to what she spoke of, he could not help but quietly admit that she was correct. "But perhaps I am mistaken and have thought too little of you," she continued, her shoulders suddenly slumping and her expression now quite forlorn. "Forgive me, Lord Hosmer. I should not think that you would be glad over my new situation as a widow."

Shock ran straight down Benedict's spine although he quickly rearranged his features so that she would not see such an expression on his face. He had not known that Lord Norwich had passed away. He had not known that Lady Norwich was now a widow and certainly, he found no joy in that knowledge.

"I thank you for your consideration, Lady Norwich," he replied, a little more quietly. Out of the corner of his eye, he saw Lady Charity bob a quick curtsey in quick farewell to the ladies she had been speaking to. His desire to go to her grew swiftly, perhaps made all the stronger by his eagerness to step away from Lady Norwich. "Now, if you will excuse me, there is a young lady that I have been eager to speak to."

A look of surprise jumped into Lady Norwich's eyes,

but Benedict paid it no attention. Instead, he bowed, turned on his heel and took his leave of her, feeling his chest fill with a great sense of relief. He had done it. He had managed to speak to Lady Norwich without any great difficulty. There was no great pain slicing through his heart, no clamoring of his terrible thoughts. Instead, there was now a quiet calmness and a sense of relief that he had managed to converse with the lady without any great difficulty and without feeling overwhelmed by his thoughts.

"Lady Charity?"

The young lady stopped at once and dropped into a quick curtsey.

"Good evening, Lord Hosmer," she said, although no smile lifted her lips and no look of delight came into her eyes. "How do you fare this evening?"

"Better than the last," he replied, bowing low and putting one hand to his heart. "I come firstly to apologize, Lady Charity, and then to ask if you would like to dance with me this evening."

He could not help but smile as Lady Charity's eyes flared with surprise, her awareness that he did not ever choose to dance at such things as this more than apparent. Benedict waited patiently, praying that she would accept him and that she would accept his apology.

"You – you wish to dance with me this evening, Lord Hosmer?" Lady Charity asked, sounding a little breathless. "Are you quite certain?"

"Indeed, I am," he professed. "You have spoken wisdom to me these last few weeks, Lady Charity, and it has taken me such a long time to, first of all listen to you, and then to act upon it. I can only apologize for my foolishness."

She swallowed and dropped her eyes for a moment.

"I saw that you spoke to Lady Norwich."

"I did," he answered, calmly. "And I am glad that I did so. I am quite determined, Lady Charity, that I shall not allow myself to dwell on what occurred in the past. I shall no longer let myself become wrapped up in pain and regret. Instead, I shall consider what is directly before me, what I might discover should I only take my eyes from the past and focus instead on what stands before me. I can only apologize, Lady Charity. Apologize that I have behaved in such a foolish and untoward manner as I have done these last few days and beg you to forgive me for my offence." He smiled at her, before dropping into another bow. "And then I should beg you to agree to step out onto the dance floor with me, Lady Charity, for I should very much like to dance with you."

Lady Charity did not say anything for some moments. Indeed, she seemed quite stunned, her eyes searching his face as though she half expected him to be telling untruths. But, it seemed, she was finally convinced for, with a small blush and a quick smile, she took her dance card from her wrist and handed it to him.

"Then yes, Lord Hosmer," she answered, filling his heart with relief and gladness. "I accept your apology and yes, I should very much like to dance with you, thank you."

CHAPTER ELEVEN

"And you found him markedly changed?"

Charity hesitated as she considered what had occurred last evening. Lord Hosmer had not only danced the quadrille with her, but also the waltz and to be in his arms had brought about such a strange swell of emotions within her heart that, even now, Charity did not want to discuss it with anyone.

"Lord Hosmer was certainly more contented, yes," she agreed, as she and Lady Hayward walked quickly towards the milliners, leaving the carriage behind them. "I confess I did see him speak to Lady Norwich and wondered what might have been said between them but, much to my astonishment, it appears as though Lord Hosmer spoke quite cordially and has no eagerness to either converse with her further or pursue a greater acquaintance."

Lady Hayward pushed open the door and stepped inside, allowing Charity to follow after her before she let the door close again. Rubbing her hands to restore a little warmth, Lady Hayward looked back at Charity.

"You did not truly believe that he might wish to reacquaint himself with her, did you?" she asked, as Charity lifted one shoulder in a half shrug. "There is too much pain there, I am sure."

"Pain that perhaps only she can remove," Charity replied, a little tersely. "But certainly, I was grateful for his apology."

"And for his dance?" Lady Hayward asked, as, much to her embarrassment, Charity felt heat climb into her cheeks. "It was noted amongst the others present that Lord Hosmer had danced with you – and only you, I might add." One eyebrow arched. "That is after he has not danced with any other young ladies for years!"

Charity looked away but could not hide her smile.

"It was very good of him," she admitted, not wanting to say anything that might reveal the truth of how she felt. "I am sure that he did so, solely to prove to me that he has every intention of doing as he said."

"Which is?"

"Which is setting his mind free of the trappings of the past," Charity replied, as they wandered a little further into the warm shop. "To forget about past hurts, to stop himself from dwelling on all that took place all those years ago and, instead, to make certain that he now finds happiness and enjoyment in what is present before him."

Lady Hayward's smile was a knowing one.

"And you were before him last evening."

"I hardly think that dancing with me meant anything

such as that," Charity declared, despite her own quickening heart and her whirling thoughts which she did not want to share with Lady Hayward at present. "He was only proving that what he has promised is to become a reality."

Lady Hayward laughed, her eyes twinkling.

"You are quite determined to believe it?" she questioned, as Charity turned her attention to silk ribbons in an attempt to change the topic of conversation. "Very well, so be it. But I will look forward to the time when you tell me that there is something more between yourself and Lord Hosmer, for then I shall be very pleased with myself indeed!"

This made Charity laugh although she had to confess quietly to herself that what Lady Hayward had said brought many thoughts to her mind. What if Lord Hosmer had, in fact, chosen to 'look at what was before him' and, in doing so, had seen her? What would she do if there *was* something more to be discovered between them? Even the thought made her heart quicken and a small smile curl her lips. She had to confess that the more she had spoken to Lord Hosmer, the more he had revealed to her, the deeper their connection had become. However, she had also felt all manner of emotions when it came to him, for he had irritated her, angered her and deeply upset her – but his apology had smoothed all hurts now that she truly believed him to be genuine in his intentions.

"Good afternoon."

Charity looked up quickly from where she had been absent-mindedly looking over silk ribbons.

"Good afternoon, Lady Dewsbury," she heard Lady Hayward reply. "You have ventured out into the cold as well, it seems!"

"Ah, yes. My daughter simply *must* have a few new things to add to her ensemble for tomorrow evening's ball," came the reply, as Charity dropped her head again and tried very hard to focus on the ribbons rather than pay attention to the conversation. "You are to attend, are you not?"

"You *are* attending, Lady Charity?"

A little startled as she was addressed by a different voice, Charity caught her breath as she looked up, only to realize that Lady Norwich had approached her on evidently stealthy feet.

"Good afternoon, Lady Norwich," she replied, quickly bobbing a curtsey. "How good to see you again."

She had not said very much to the lady other than to greet her and to make meaningless conversation during the dinner party some time ago, making her a little surprised that Lady Norwich now approached her in such a manner.

"Are you attending Lord Livingstone's ball, Lady Charity?" Lady Norwich asked, a hardness appearing in her voice that sounded a warning in Charity's mind. "I should very much like to know."

A little confused as to why the lady might wish to know such a thing, Charity gave her a small nod.

"I see." Lady Norwich lifted her chin and, for the first time, Charity noticed just how cold the lady's blue eyes could be. "I suspect that Lord Hosmer will be present also."

"I could not say," Charity answered, growing more and more uncomfortable with every moment that passed. "But I should not expect him to have refused such an invitation." She tried to smile at the lady but Lady Norwich's expression remained impassive. "Might I ask if there is any particular reason for your question?"

Her glance slid towards Lady Hayward but her companion was still deep in conversation with Lady Dewsbury and did not notice Charity's quick glance.

"I did notice, Lady Charity, that Lord Hosmer danced with you last evening," Lady Norwich replied, her chin still lifted as though she was trying to look down her nose at Charity in an attempt to intimidate her. "Twice."

Charity blinked rapidly, trying to assess what the lady meant.

"That is so," she answered, slowly. "I was very glad indeed to step out with him."

Lady Norwich's lips flattened for a moment and she looked away, drawing in a great breath as though she were attempting to rein in whatever anger now filled her.

"You will not be aware, Lady Charity – or mayhap you will, if Lord Hosmer has told you so – that he refused to step out with me."

"I did not know," Charity answered swiftly, feeling a little dazed at the furious words being thrown at her but quite determined to stand up for herself. "I do not think that Lord Hosmer even contemplated sharing such information with me, Lady Norwich. He would have no reason to."

Taking a small step forward, Lady Norwich's eyes

narrowed as she pointed one finger in Charity's direction. Heat poured into Charity's face as she forced herself to hold Lady Norwich's gaze, refusing to look away despite how much clear anger and ire was being thrust towards her.

"Why, might I ask, would he dance with you when he had only just refused to do so with me?" she hissed, clearly infuriated. "I asked him specifically if he was to dance and he said he was not willing to do so! And then, within the next hour, I saw him take your arm and lead you out with him, to dance first the cotillion, I believe and then, much later on, the waltz!"

"I cannot speak for Lord Hosmer," Charity replied, aware of the slight tremor in her voice but refusing to permit Lady Norwich's anger to shake her any more than it had thus far. "All I can tell you is that he asked if I should like to dance and I accepted him. That is all."

For whatever reason, this statement seemed to inflate Lady Norwich's anger all the more. Her cheeks went scarlet, her eyes blazed with fury and she shook her finger towards Charity with a good deal more vehemence.

"Then it is you!" she stated, still keeping her voice low but unable to hide the vehemence. "It is you that I must remove from his sphere! I will not have it, Lady Charity. I will not have it!"

And with that said, she turned on her heel and flounced towards the other side of the shop, leaving Charity to stare after her in shock. She had very little idea as to why Lady Norwich appeared to be so upset with her and certainly had even less understanding as to what Lady Norwich meant when it came to Lord Hosmer, but still, the encounter had shaken her.

Behind her, she heard Lady Hayward laugh at something Lady Dewsbury said, and the sound rattled through her core, hard and brash against the shock that she felt. Had Lady Dewsbury deliberately gone to speak to Lady Hayward, so that her daughter might address Charity? Or had it been sheer good fortune on Lady Norwich's part?

"Lady Charity?"

Charity jumped as Lady Hayward's voice reached her and she turned around to see the lady look at her in surprise.

"Are you quite all right?"

Charity nodded, her throat tight.

"I – I should like to go elsewhere, Lady Hayward," she said, keeping her voice low and forcing herself not to look around the shop for Lady Norwich. "Might we take our leave?"

There was a look of surprise in Lady Hayward's eyes but, after a moment, she nodded her agreement.

"But of course," she said, turning back towards the door. "There is another shop only a few yards away. If you are willing to walk, then we can be there within a few minutes, or if you would like to return to the carriage, then –"

"I will be quite contented to walk," Charity replied hastily, wanting nothing more than to depart from the shop at once. "Please, lead on, Lady Hayward."

It was not until they were outside, back into the frosty

air under grey skies that Lady Hayward finally asked Charity what had happened.

"Lady Norwich spoke to me," Charity answered, keeping her head lowered so that the wind would not manage to spread its icy fingers around the back of her neck. "She spoke of Lord Hosmer. She asked why he would dance with me when only a few minutes earlier, she had been refused by him."

Lady Hayward frowned but said nothing until they had entered the second milliner's shop which, much to Charity's relief, was quite empty save for the proprietor who greeted them warmly.

"And why would she do such a thing?" Lady Hayward asked, as Charity shook her head, the tension beginning to fade from her. "Why would she be upset about Lord Hosmer's rejection of her, given all that has passed between them?"

"I do not know," Charity replied, honestly. "But needless to say, I was rather taken aback by her sharp words. It was as though she blamed me for his choice in some way, as though I am the one responsible! There was a good deal of anger there and it was directed solely towards me."

"That is very strange indeed," Lady Hayward answered, looking at Charity carefully. "I do hope you are not at all upset by it."

Charity closed her eyes for a moment and drew in a long breath.

"I confess that I was," she admitted, as Lady Hayward's eyes filled with concern. "She stated that she holds me solely responsible, although quite what I am responsible for, I could not say! I fear that there will be some sort of consequence brought to bear, given the depths of her ire."

"Then you must speak of it to Lord Hosmer," Lady Hayward replied, firmly. "You must tell him what has occurred and state the truth of your feelings. I am quite certain that he will have no knowledge of what Lady Norwich said and will be quite taken aback by it all. But I believe it to be imperative that he is aware of what she has said, given that it has been expressed so strongly."

Charity nodded in agreement, the final wisps of strain and upset leaving her as she took in Lady Hayward's practical words.

"I shall do so," she agreed, as Lady Hayward smiled quietly. "Whenever I am next in his company, I shall make it my sole purpose."

"That will be at the ball, I presume?" Lady Hayward asked, one eyebrow lifting as Charity nodded. "I wonder if he will ask you to dance again, Lady Charity." Her smile grew. "Will you be glad to accept him?"

Hesitating in her response, Charity considered all that Lady Norwich had said.

"I will not permit Lady Norwich to dictate what I can or cannot do," she replied, speaking with as much confidence as she could. "If he should ask me then yes, I will accept him. Although, I confess I wonder what Lady Norwich will think, should she see such a thing occurring again."

"And what the *ton* might think also," Lady Hayward added, as Charity flushed. "You must be careful now,

Lady Charity. There is more to this matter than I think either of us are fully aware of."

"So it would seem," Charity agreed, softly. "I will be careful, Lady Hayward. Very careful indeed."

"MY LADY, YOU HAVE A VISITOR."

Charity looked up from her needlework in surprise, turning her head to glance out of the window and confirming to herself that yes, the snow was falling very heavily indeed. It had been doing so for most of the morning and now, given that it was the afternoon, she had not expected there to be any afternoon callers.

"Might I ask who?" she said, as the butler came forward with the gentleman's card.

"Lord Hosmer, my Lady," came the reply, as Charity picked up the card and saw his name printed there. "What shall I say to him?"

Charity considered for a moment. Lady Hayward had gone to her room to rest for a short time and, whilst Charity could very easily call a maid to come to join her, it would be best for her to have her chaperone present.

"Ask him to join me," Charity replied, after a few moments. "And bring in one of the maids." She held up one hand, preventing the butler from departing. "Make certain that one of the staff goes to Lady Hayward. If she is able to come and join us, then that would be preferable. However, if she is asleep, then I should not like her woken."

"Of course, my Lady."

"Have a tea tray brought also," Charity finished, as the butler nodded. "And quickly if you please. Lord Hosmer will, I am sure, be very cold indeed."

The butler nodded and departed, leaving Charity to sit quietly and wait for Lord Hosmer to join her. A flood of nervousness poured into her as she sat in silence, although whether it was in the knowledge that she would have to tell Lord Hosmer about Lady Norwich or simply because she would be in his company again? After what Lady Hayward had suggested about there being a greater intimacy between herself and Lord Hosmer than perhaps, at present, she was a little more aware of his presence and the emotions that were slowly beginning to be stirred up within her.

Trying her best not to consider such things, for fear that she would look flustered and embarrassed by the time Lord Hosmer arrived, Charity drew in long, steadying breaths, just as the maid came in and scurried to sit in the corner, whilst another brought in a tea tray in preparation for Lord Hosmer's entrance. Charity rose to her feet as the door opened for what was now the third time, her eyes fixing to his almost at the moment he entered.

"Good afternoon, Lord Hosmer," she said, dropping into a curtsey. "Lady Hayward is resting at present but I hope that she will join us soon."

Lord Hosmer rose from his bow and smiled at her.

"I quite understand," he said, as he made his way to the chair which she directed him to. "I am sorry for calling so unexpectedly, but I could not simply remain at home for the rest of the day. I have found a new enjoyment in being in London at the present season - a circumstance that I blame you for entirely, Lady Charity, although I am very grateful for it also."

"I am glad to hear it, Lord Hosmer," Charity replied, reaching to pour the tea. "I am sure you are a little cold, however. Might I offer you some tea?"

"Yes, thank you," he answered, accepting the cup from her with a warm smile. "You have not ventured out, I suppose?"

This seemed like the perfect opportunity for her to mention her interaction with Lady Norwich and, despite the nervous anticipation that filled her, Charity was quite determined to do so. She could not imagine what he would say – for he might brush off the conversation as nothing more than foolishness on Lady Norwich's part, but still, she wanted him to know of it. "Both myself and Lady Hayward went to the milliners yesterday," she said, as Lord Hosmer took a sip of his tea. "I - I had an encounter with Lady Norwich."

Lord Hosmer looked at her for a moment before his brow began to furrow and he set his teacup back in its saucer.

"Might I ask if this was a welcome meeting?" he asked. "From the look on your face, I would expect you to state that it was not so."

"I wish I could say otherwise, Lord Hosmer, but you are correct, it was not welcome," Charity replied, a trifle tentatively. "I was hoping to speak to you of it tomorrow evening at the ball, but it is good that we have the opportunity to do so now. I feel it only fair to warn you that I believe Lady Norwich still has..." She bit her lip, not quite certain how to express it. "She was greatly distressed that you had stepped out on the dance floor with me but had not done so with her." The look of shock which appeared on Lord Hosmer's face told Charity that she had been right to speak of such a thing to him. His expression was almost frozen, his eyes holding tight to hers as though he was uncertain of whether or not she spoke the truth. "Lady Norwich appeared to blame me for that circumstance, Lord Hosmer," Charity finished, spreading her hands. "I know not why."

She held his gaze steadily, growing a little perturbed by his lack of response. Why had he not said something to her as yet? Why had he not immediately remarked that there was naught but foolishness in Lady Norwich's suggestion? Surely he was not delighted to hear of Lady Norwich's upset? Whilst she knew that Lady Norwich had hurt him greatly, Charity had never once thought that he would be callous enough to hope that, one day, he might be able to do the very same to Lady Norwich in retaliation!

"Lord Hosmer?" Her voice was quiet now, tension tightening her frame as she leaned a little further forward in her chair, seeing how he began to blink rapidly, shaking his head as he did so. "I did not mean to –"

"Forgive me, Lady Charity." Lord Hosmer tried to smile but she could see that it did not reach his eyes. "What you have told me has come as something of a shock, I confess. I never once expected to hear that she...." Again, he shook his head and let out a long, slow breath as he did so. "She was upset that I refused to dance with her? Truly?"

"Yes," Charity replied, seeing a flash of anger in his eyes. "I was, I confess, a little surprised by such a thing but she appeared to be quite determined in her accusation."

"An accusation that you were to blame for my decision?" he asked, as Charity nodded. "How very odd." His anger faded as he looked back at her. "I am sorry for that, Lady Charity."

A little relieved that he had finally spoken and that he was not in any way seeming to justify Lady Norwich's outburst, Charity shook her head.

"It is not your fault in any way, Lord Hosmer," she replied, honestly. "I am only glad that I was able to speak to you of this, for I cannot be certain of what she intends."

"It sounds very much as though she intends to make certain our acquaintance is renewed, just as it was before," he replied, looking now a little grim. "To pretend that all is well, that nothing has altered between us."

Charity nodded slowly, seeing the frustration in his eyes.

"I am sorry if I have made things at all difficult for you."

"No, no!" His exclamation came quickly and he rose from his chair. Much to her astonishment, he came towards her and, not quite certain what else she ought to do, Charity found herself on her feet, now standing rather close to him. "Forgive my vehemence but I cannot permit you to *ever* believe that you are the one who has done wrong," he said, reaching out and taking her hand in his. Charity swallowed hard. "You have attempted to show me the joy and the happiness that can be found at this time of year, Lady Charity," he continued, still speaking with great fervor and eagerness. "You have sought to encourage me when I have been determined to remain in darkness and, had it not been for you, I am quite certain that I would have lingered on in such a fashion for a very long time indeed." His thumb rubbed across the back of her hand and Charity caught her breath, her whole body seeming to burn with a sudden and furious heat. "I can listen to the songs of Christmas being sung and find delight in them, rather than permitting myself to be taken back to a more melancholy time. I can look out at the snow and..." He trailed off, tilting his head just a little as he looked at her. "I can look out at the snow and, rather than see Lady Frederica telling me that all was at an end, I see a young lady standing by the window, looking out at the snow and smiling with such evident delight that my heart begins to yearn to capture that beauty and happiness for myself. I have begun to find a new path, Lady Charity, and that has been entirely due to you. How can you then think that there might be something wrong in your actions? You must never, *never* permit yourself to believe so. I shall not permit it."

This long speech came to a sudden end as he lifted her hand and pressed his lips to it. Such was the force of emotion that swept through her at his action, at the feel of his lips against her hand, that Charity swayed slightly for a moment, almost entirely overcome by all that she felt. When he lifted his head to look into her eyes, the urge to step a little closer so that she might be all the nearer to him seemed to push her in forward – only for the door to open and Lord Hosmer to quickly step back.

"*Do* forgive me, Lord Hosmer."

Charity took a small step back as Lady Hayward entered the room, praying that her chaperone had not seen precisely just how near Lord Hosmer had been to her – nor that his lips had been pressed against her hand.

"There is nothing to forgive, Lady Hayward," Lord Hosmer replied, with a small bow. "I called unexpectedly and did not even have the decency to send a note first to inform you of my intentions!"

"But it seems now that I have missed your visit entirely," Lady Hayward replied, with a quick smile, although her eyes caught Charity's and, instantly, Charity was aware of just how much heat spiraled through her at the look. Evidently, Lady Hayward was either aware of, or a little suspicious of, what had taken place between Charity and Lord Hosmer during her absence. "Have you taken tea with Lady Charity already?"

"I have," Lord Hosmer replied, glancing back at Charity, who could not, for whatever reason, look into his face given the swell of embarrassment which was now rising slowly in her chest. "But if you would like me to stay a little longer in order to converse, Lady Hayward, then I would be very glad to do so. I should not want you to feel in any way neglected, Lady Hayward."

Much to Charity's relief, Lady Hayward only laughed and waved a hand at him.

"Now you are being much too generous, Lord Hosmer," she answered, as Charity managed a small smile. "I shall not keep you. You are to be at the ball tomorrow evening, however?"

"I am," Lord Hosmer replied. "And I am, for what is

the first time in a very long while, eagerly looking forward to it." Another glance towards Charity told her that she was the cause of such a change in his heart and Charity could not help but smile back at him, feeling both relief and gladness that he had been so changed. "And there will be a great many dances, wonderful entertainment and, from what I have heard, quieter rooms where singing and various other entertainments will take place. Lord Livingstone is a gentleman who does not spare any expense!"

"It sounds quite wonderful," Charity replied, her heart already filling with excitement at Lord Hosmer's description.

"And you will make certain to dance with me, I hope?"

The blush that warmed her cheeks was more than obvious, but still, Charity's smile remained.

"I should be very glad to do so, Lord Hosmer."

His eyes flickered as he smiled back at her, perhaps recalling what had been shared between them before Lady Hayward's interruption.

"Wonderful," he replied, bowing low. "Until tomorrow then, Lady Charity."

"I look forward to seeing you again, Lord Hosmer," Charity replied, speaking honestly. "Good afternoon."

CHAPTER TWELVE

B enedict's brow furrowed as he made his way into the ballroom.

"You do not look particularly happy, given that we are now stepping into what is certain to be a most excellent and enjoyable evening," Ramsbury remarked, one brow lifted. "Christmas Day is a very short time away and this is one of the most enjoyable evenings of the Season! Although," he added, a small smile tugging at his lips, "from what I recall, last year you stayed only a short while and then made your way to Whites."

"Pray, do not remind me of such foolishness," Benedict replied, with a small shake of his head. "This year, I am quite determined to find all manner of enjoyment."

"Then might I suggest that you remove that frown from your face?" Ramsbury replied, with a chuckle. "Otherwise it may appear that, despite your supposed eagerness and delight, those around you will believe that you are quite out of sorts!"

Making a great effort to rearrange his features, Benedict let out a long breath and looked to his friend, seeing how Lady Ramsbury had already fallen into conversation with another acquaintance. "It seems that Lady Norwich has spoken to Lady Charity and stated, quite clearly, I might add, that she was most displeased that I chose to dance with Lady Charity and, at the same time, refused her."

Ramsbury's genial smile faded in an instant.

"What can you mean?"

"It is just as I have said," Benedict told him. "Lady Norwich appears to blame Lady Charity for the fact that I will not dance with her. I am rather surprised to hear such a thing, of course, but I do not disbelieve Lady Charity, of course." He frowned again, despite himself. "It seems rather odd, given that Lady Norwich and I are only briefly reacquainted. Indeed, we have only had one very small conversation and I made it quite plain to her, I am sure, that I have no wish to further our acquaintance in any way."

"Quite understandable, and wise," Ramsbury agreed. "So why then should she have such discontent if you would not dance with her?"

"That is something which has laid heavily on my mind ever since Lady Charity informed me of it," Benedict replied. "And whilst I am very eager indeed to see what this evening will bring, I am also a little perturbed."

"You are concerned that Lady Norwich will approach you and say something?" Ramsbury asked, now looking a little confused. "Surely such a conversation, whilst a little awkward, mayhap, is no great cause for concern?"

Pausing for a moment, Benedict nodded and then shrugged.

"I do not know what it is that Lady Norwich wants," he said, truthfully. "I believe that is what concerns me the most. Although I made quite plain to Lady Charity that I had no interest in furthering an acquaintance with Lady Norwich, no matter what the lady in question might suggest by making statements such as that!"

Ramsbury chuckled.

"That is also wise, Hosmer," he answered, as Benedict gave him a wry smile. "I believe that you would not wish to do anything at all to injure your current acquaintance with Lady Charity. Am I right in suggesting so?"

Benedict did not hesitate.

"You are quite correct," he stated, recalling silently just how he had kissed her hand and how such a small action had filled him with great waves of emotion. He not only appreciated her, valued her and thought well of her, there was a closeness beginning to form between them that he simply could not depart from. Indeed, the only urge within him was to further their acquaintance all the more and, in fact, to consider what might now be before him should he only dare grasp it. Lady Charity had shown him the joy and the happiness that could be found in not only the little Season but also in the excitement that came in the days before Christmas and for that, Benedict wanted always to show her just how much she had come to mean to him.

"Then might I suggest that you go to speak to her at this very moment?" Ramsbury asked, nudging Benedict with his elbow. "And perhaps steal the supper dance?"

Benedict grinned at his friend, all concern – for the moment – gone from his mind.

"An excellent suggestion," he replied, as Ramsbury chuckled. "Do excuse me."

Benedict knew the moment that Lady Charity saw him, for her eyes flared and a small blush warmed her cheeks as she darted her gaze away for just a moment, in a clear attempt to make certain that those she spoke to at present did not think poorly of her. A smile crossed his face as he continued towards her, already thinking of what it would be like to waltz with her again. After their closeness the previous day, before Lady Hayward had interrupted them, Benedict had felt himself yearning for something more, something that would not fade but would only grow stronger.

"Good evening, Lady Charity," he began, just as the gentleman and the lady that she had been conversing with excused themselves from her and Lady Hayward. "And good evening Lady Hayward. What an excellent evening this is!"

Lady Charity laughed, her eyes sparkling.

"How marked a change there is in you, Lord Hosmer!" she answered, with a bright smile. "I am sure that last Christmas time, you would not have found such enjoyment!"

He grinned at her.

"Indeed, it would have been just as you have described, Lady Charity. Ramsbury will tell you the truth of it all, should you ask him! I was, most likely, very poor company, and would not have lingered long in the ballroom. Instead, I believe I went in search of card games and the like before returning home rather early!"

"But not this evening, I hope," Lady Hayward asked, a knowing look in her eyes.

Benedict inclined his head.

"I intend to do the very opposite," he informed her. "Lady Charity, might you be willing to present me with your dance card? I should like to steal two of your dances, if I may?"

Lady Charity handed it to him without hesitation.

"But of course, Lord Hosmer."

Relief crowded his heart as he saw that her supper dance was still available to him, as well as a few others. Swiftly he wrote his name for the supper dance and the country dance, knowing that he would have to wait for some time for the supper dance but trusting that it would be worth the wait.

"The country dance and the supper dance, Lady Charity," he murmured, handing it back to her. "If that would suit you?"

"It would suit me very well, Lord Hosmer, thank you," came the quiet reply, her fingers brushing his as she took back the dance card. "I look forward to our dances."

"As do I," he replied, a deep sense of contentment filling him. "As do I, Lady Charity."

"It is close to the time for the supper dance, is it not?"

Lady Ramsbury laughed and put one hand on Benedict's arm.

"I do not believe that I have ever seen you so eager, Lord Hosmer," she said, as Benedict looked away, a little embarrassed. "Can it be that you might now be considering courtship with Lady Charity?"

"I shall hide nothing from you," Benedict replied, quietly. "I have every intention of courting Lady Charity. In fact, I would admit to considering a little *more* than that, if I were being entirely truthful with you. She is the most wonderful of young ladies and I do not think that I would ever have found such joy again, were it not for her."

Lady Ramsbury's smile was gentle and Benedict knew that she was truly glad to hear him speak so.

"I think Lady Charity is an excellent choice, Lord Hosmer," she answered, quietly. "And I have no doubt that she will accept you, whatever you may choose to ask her! I have seen the look in her eyes when she is with you, the smile that your mere presence brings to her. There is an intimacy between you both that has become more than apparent and I am truly happy at such a development. It will bring you *both* a great happiness, I am certain."

"I believe it will," Benedict replied, a smile on his face that he could not seem to remove. "And now, if you will excuse me, I must go in search of the lady. I have been looking forward to this dance for most of the evening!"

Lady Ramsbury laughed and pressed his arm gently before he stepped away, making his way through the crowd and hearing the laughter and the delight that came from the other guests. With Christmas Day only a short time away, there seemed now to be a fresh happiness in Benedict's heart that he was certain would never fade for as long as he was with Lady Charity. The air might be chilly with the snow still falling, but the warmth that was in his heart was blazing with heat. And it was all thanks to Lady Charity.

"Lord Hosmer?"

He stopped suddenly, just as Lady Norwich stepped in front of him. Her eyes were fixed on his, her lips thin and there was a tightness about her frame which spoke of a great deal of tension.

"Lady Norwich," he said, his smile fading. "Do excuse me. I have no intention of being rude but I am engaged for the supper dance and should not like to be tardy."

He made to step past her but Lady Norwich took a small side step and forced herself in front of him.

"You refused to dance with *me*, Lord Hosmer."

A little surprised, Benedict spread his hands.

"As I have every right to do," he replied, as calmly as he could. "Forgive me, Lady Norwich, but I –"

"You must."

Her insistence began to irritate him.

"I have heard from Lady Charity what you spoke of," he said, relieved now that he had chosen to make his way to Lady Charity's side well in advance of the supper dance beginning. "I do not understand it, Lady Norwich and I will absolve you at this very moment of any hope that you might have of any sort of renewed acquaintance between us."

Lady Norwich shook her head, her face now a little white.

"I will not accept any such statement from you, Lord Hosmer," she answered, firmly. "There was once an intimacy between us. An intimacy that I believe can be established again!"

Benedict stared at the lady in shock, his heart thumping furiously. Whatever could she mean? There was not even a single thought of such a thing in his mind and yet it seemed that Lady Norwich had been hoping for precisely that!

"That is why I have returned to London!" Lady Norwich exclaimed, as Benedict began to shake his head. "I have been eagerly hoping that you would look upon me again with favor. I know that I made an unwise choice in setting aside what had been agreed between us and, instead, making my way to another, but I have had time to reflect on such a decision and can only feel regret as to my foolishness. My late husband did not care for me, not in the way that I knew you once did, proven entirely by his lack of consideration for me in his will." She drew in a shaky breath. "If only you could –"

"I have no interest in considering any sort of acquaintance, Lady Norwich," Benedict interrupted, speaking as loudly as he dared. "Why you should think so, I cannot imagine!"

"Because I know that you still must care for me," Lady Norwich said, beseechingly. "I have heard that you have returned to London every Christmas and have been melancholy and utterly distraught!"

Benedict grimaced but took a small step back from her.

"That may be so, but that has been *my* foolishness," he declared, as Lady Norwich's eyes began to glisten with tears. "To my immense relief, I have discovered a new happiness which has pulled me from such things." Glancing to his right and to his left, he finally caught sight of Lady Charity, seeing how she looked back at him, a glimmer of uncertainty in her expression. "I danced with Lady Charity because I have a desire to be in her company, Lady Norwich." Turning his gaze back towards the lady in question, he fixed his gaze to hers, praying that she would listen to everything he said and realize that he was quite serious with all that he was about to say. "I have no desire to be in your company for any great length of time. The intimacy which was between us was shattered the moment that you chose to step away from me and I have no interest in securing it again. I have found a new happiness, a new joy and a new contentment that I believe I would never have truly discovered should we have wed. I had believed that you cared for me, but I soon realized just how mistaken I was. But I shall not have such doubts or fears with Lady Charity. I trust her implicitly and the care that she has shown me proves what is in her heart. Remove such thoughts from your mind, Lady Norwich. Throw any hope from your heart. It shall never be fulfilled."

Benedict stepped away from her, his head inclining for just a moment before he began to walk towards Lady Charity. His heart was quiet and calm, for he had spoken with honesty and distinction, not having any urge to injure Lady Norwich with what he had said but rather, instead, to speak in such a way that there could not be any doubt. The look in her eyes had been one of pain and of sorrow but Benedict had not allowed her emotions to affect him. It seemed that the late Lord Norwich had not cared for her in the way that Lady Norwich had expected and him leaving her with very little in his will, Benedict knew, must be very difficult for the lady indeed. Regardless, Benedict remained utterly steadfast. She needed to understand that there could be nothing between them. It was not his duty nor his responsibility to care for her now.

"Lady Charity." Reaching out one hand as though he needed to feel her touch, Benedict smiled at her with both relief and gladness as she accepted it. "Might we step out for the supper dance? I have been –"

"You have promised the dance to me!"

Benedict frowned hard and turned his head. Lady Norwich was approaching him, her face set and, much to his dismay, her mother alongside her.

"I have done no such thing, Lady Norwich," Benedict replied, firmly. "Pray, do not –"

"Your name is written on my dance card."

Benedict sighed and closed his eyes for a moment, before looking to Lady Charity with a small, wry smile.

"Shall we, Lady Charity?" he asked again, ignoring Lady Norwich entirely. "The supper dance is, as you know, the one I have been greatly anticipating."

"I do not think so, Lord Hosmer!" Lady Dewsbury exclaimed, loudly. "You have promised this dance to my daughter. Your name is written here, on her dance card!"

Lady Charity's hand pulled from his.

"You have only just finished speaking to me of your eagerness to set things right between us, Lord Hosmer," Lady Norwich said, plaintively. "I am sure that you saw him conversing with me at length, Lady Charity, did you not? Do you wish to know what he spoke of?"

Benedict turned a hard gaze to Lady Norwich.

"Do not attempt to tell untruths, Lady Norwich," he said, becoming a little angry now. "I –"

"You stated, quite plainly, that you wished to make things right between us," she interrupted, as Lady Charity began to frown. "Of course, you said just how glad you were for Lady Charity's contribution to your recovered happiness but that, knowing there was now opportunity for a re-establishing of our acquaintance, you could not help but feel all the more contented. I quite understand if you have not spoken to Lady Charity of this as yet, but the dance is to be mine."

This was evidently confirmed by the waving of her dance card in front of his face where, Benedict noted, his name *was* written.

"I did not write my name there," he said, his heart beginning to pound as he looked from Lady Norwich to Lady Charity and saw her frown. "That is..." He did not want to say outright that Lady Norwich had done so deliberately but prayed that Lady Charity would realize that. Unfortunately for him, it also appeared as though Lady Norwich's outburst had caught the attention of one or two others, for a small group had begun to form around them, making him all the more reluctant to speak poorly of Lady Norwich's behavior. At the same time, however, he did not want to abandon Lady Charity and was quite determined to step out with her. "Lady Charity, shall we - ?"

"Lord Hosmer!" Lady Dewsbury's tone was sharp, catching even more attention from the other guests. "You cannot deny my daughter what you have promised! I am sure that Lady Charity will understand! What was once between you has, understandably, begun to form again and other friendships and acquaintances that have been formed –" she sent a sharp look towards Lady Charity, "must now be pushed to the side."

Benedict shook his head, feeling anger begin to burn within his heart. He was not about to allow Lady Dewsbury and Lady Norwich to manipulate him in such a manner, to try and set himself and Lady Charity asunder when he had only just discovered happiness again! He could not understand Lady Norwich's reasons for doing so, could not make sense of why she had chosen to do such a thing and yet, standing in the middle of a crowd of guests – all of whom were now looking at him – Benedict found himself quite uncertain as to what was best to say.

"If you will excuse us."

Lady Hayward's voice reached Benedict's ears and he turned to see her taking Lady Charity's arm and bodily beginning to move them both away from this scene.

"Please, Lady Hayward, I –"

"Do excuse us."

Her words were firm, her eyes hard and the way she looked at Benedict made him wither inside. Lady Charity had not turned her head back towards him, had not so much as glanced at him and the urge within him to go to her, to reach out to her and pull her to him was practically overwhelming. But before he could say a word, Lady Charity was gone, disappearing into the ether of crowd.

"And the supper dance has just been announced," Lady Norwich declared, with a sense of great satisfaction in her voice. "Shall we, Lord Hosmer?"

Fury filled him.

"No, Lady Norwich," he said, vehemently. "We are *not* to dance this evening. I *have* not written my name on your dance card. I have *not* made any suggestion that we reacquaint ourselves and I have *certainly* not ever even thought of an intimacy between us. Whatever you have begun to believe, I can assure you, you are quite mistaken!" His voice was rising now but Benedict could not help but speak with determination and passion, wanting to make it quite clear with both Lady Norwich and those now listening that there was to be no restarting of any acquaintance between them. "Excuse me."

He heard Lady Norwich begin to protest but Benedict could not allow himself to listen. Walking swiftly, but doing all he could to keep his composure and his expression steady, Benedict made his way through the ballroom and towards the door. This night, the evening he had been looking forward to, had suddenly become one of the most disastrous nights of his life - and all he could think of was Lady Charity. Where was she? And just what would she now be thinking of him?

CHAPTER THIRTEEN

"How are you, my dear?"

Charity gave Lady Hayward a wan smile. Last evening had not gone as she had expected and the embarrassment of what had occurred lingered with her still.

"I am..."

She trailed off, not quite certain how to answer the lady. What was it she felt at present? Yes, she had been caught by embarrassment last evening, to the point that Lady Hayward had thought it best they step away from the scene, but that had not been what had kept her from sleep. There was, unfortunately, a small niggle of doubt in her heart which would not leave her, no matter what she attempted.

"Sit down and let me fetch you some tea," Lady Hayward said, as Charity realized she had done nothing other than stand after entering the room, rather than sit down anywhere. "Come over by the fire."

Charity did as she was asked, seating herself by the fire and allowing the warmth to spread over her.

"I can imagine that you must be a little troubled after last evening," Lady Hayward said, handing Charity a teacup and saucer. "For Lady Norwich to behave like that was utterly disgraceful!"

Charity bit her lip and looked away, her eyes drawn to the flames which burned merrily in the grate. She watched the yellow and the orange meld together, occasionally seeing a flash of blue where the heat was at its height – and allowed herself to speak the words that had been lingering in her mind.

"I did see him speak to Lady Norwich at length, before he approached me."

Her voice was quiet, her words holding no strength, but when she glanced at Lady Hayward, Charity saw there was a deep frown beginning to form on the lady's face.

"That may be so, Lady Charity, but surely you cannot imagine that there was even a modicum of truth in what Lady Norwich said?" Lady Hayward asked, leaning forward to pick up her own teacup. "The lady is clearly quite determined to regain Lord Hosmer's acquaintance, for whatever reason, but I do not think that there is *any* such desire on his part."

"I want to believe that it is so," Charity replied, finding it difficult to explain all that she felt, "but there is a part of me which realizes the truth of the matter."

"Which is?" Lady Hayward prompted, one eyebrow arched.

"Which is that there was a strong bond between Lord

Hosmer and Lady Norwich," Charity answered, a tightness squeezing her heart painfully. "He has been lost these last few years because of her absence, because of her choice. The pain he felt has lingered and he had chosen to remain there, clearly distraught over what occurred. When the chance is offered to him to return to her side, might there not be some possibility that he would do so, given how strongly he felt for her?"

Lady Hayward paused for a moment, her head tilting just a little as she looked at Charity.

"Do you truly believe that, Charity?" she asked, as Charity dropped her head, feeling all the more embarrassed. "Is there a part of you which thinks such a thing might be true?"

"There is," Charity admitted, speaking so quietly that she knew Lady Hayward would struggle to hear her. "I confess that what Lady Dewsbury said, in particular, has not yet left my thoughts."

"I see." Lady Hayward let out a long breath, then shook her head. "Lady Charity," she continued, after a few moments. "Allow me to remind you of the scene that I walked into only a few days ago. Lord Hosmer had taken your hand, I believe. I do not know precisely what had passed between you, but it was something of significance, was it not?" Charity blushed and nodded, instantly recalling the moment that Lord Hosmer had lifted her hand to his lips, as a fleeting warmth began to spread through her heart, only to fade again in a few moments. "Do you truly believe that a gentleman who is clearly so very eager to continue to further his acquaintance with you will, in fact, then return to a lady who has done him naught but harm?" Lady Hayward asked, quietly. "He has been so very grateful to you for pulling him from his sadness and his sorrow. He has told you so on multiple occasions and there has been such a change in his demeanor which speaks of only the truth of such a change. There is a good deal more to your acquaintance than I believe there ever was with Lady Norwich. Do not turn away from him now, Lady Charity. Allow what has occurred between you to remind you of the truth of his heart – and look into your own to discover it there also. Hold onto what can be yours and reject the doubts and fears that fling themselves at you, for those worries and anxieties are precisely what Lady Dewsbury and her manipulative daughter want you to consider." Her expression darkened and she looked away for a moment, clearly struggling to keep her manner calm and supportive – or perhaps fighting against the urge to speak all the more strongly about Lady Norwich herself. "Perhaps we ought to call upon Lord Hosmer, Lady Charity. Or mayhap you might write to him. Either way, do not allow silence to linger between you. Silence will bring nothing more but doubts and fears, instead of resolution and understanding. If you are hopeful that this matter might be resolved, then find a way to approach him, so that you might hear the truth from his lips and allow yourself, finally, to trust him."

Charity let out a long, slow breath and nodded, swallowing the lump in her throat and praying that she would not let tears fall. Turning her head to look back into the flames, she settled her shoulders and told herself that Lady Hayward was quite correct – that if she could trust what had passed between herself and Lord Hosmer in the past, then she would lose her doubts and her fears. Lord Hosmer *had* told her, many times, that he was more than grateful to her, had been glad to leave his sorrow and his pain behind. Was she about to dismiss all that, simply because Lady Norwich and Lady Dewsbury told her so? A small, creeping confidence began to steal over her heart as she considered this, realizing that all Lady Hayward had said was quite correct.

"I will," she said aloud, looking back at Lady Hayward. "You are right, Lady Hayward. I have let all that Lady Dewsbury said and all that I know occurred between Lord Hosmer and Lady Norwich in the past, flood my thoughts and push fears and doubts into my heart. I have forgotten what he has said and what has been shared between us. But I shall do so no longer." Her lips pulled into a small smile and the tears which had threatened began to fade away as a renewed confidence filled her heart. "Thank you, Lady Hayward."

"But of course," Lady Hayward replied, now looking rather relieved. "So, shall you write to him?"

"I shall –"

Charity's answer was cut off by a quiet knock on the drawing room door. Calling for the servant to enter, Charity was all the more astonished when the butler informed them both that there were visitors waiting to be permitted to see them.

"And who has called?" Lady Hayward asked, sending a quick look towards Charity, who found herself hoping that it was none other than Lord Hosmer come to speak to her. "It is still very cold and, from what I can see, snowing outside! They must have been very eager indeed to call upon us!"

Her eyes twinkled as she smiled at Charity, only for that smile to fix in place as the butler spoke the visitors' names.

"I see."

Charity's heart slammed hard against her chest, her stomach tightening and a deep frown beginning to form across her brow.

"Well," Lady Hayward continued, as she considered, "it would be rude indeed to refuse to see them." Her gaze turned back to Charity's for a moment, looking at her steadily. "But what do you think, Lady Charity? I will refuse to allow them to call, if you would prefer it."

Taking in a steadying breath, Charity lifted her chin and looked back at the butler.

"Of course, they must be permitted to call," she said, speaking with more confidence than she truly felt. "And a fresh tea tray will need to be brought, if you please."

The butler nodded and excused himself and Charity could only look helplessly after him, feeling all manner of nervousness flood her.

"Why should they wish to call, after what happened last evening?" Lady Hayward asked, her voice holding a faint trace of anger. "Do not listen to a word that they say, Lady Charity, I beg you. No doubt, Lady Dewsbury will do much the same as last evening and Lady Norwich will attempt to convince you that there is a connection between herself and Lord Hosmer which can never be broken." Her eyes held Charity's firmly. "Do not allow them to convince you of it."

"I – I will not," Charity answered, forcing herself to find the same strength of resolve that had been present within her spirits only a short time before. "Lord Hosmer is not here to either argue or defend himself, which means that I must do it on his behalf." Her fingers twisted together as she set her shoulders. "They will not convince me, Lady Hayward. Not after what you have said. I can assure you of that."

Lady Hayward looked all the more pleased, although there was a flicker of anger in her eyes that only grew rather than faded.

"I am very glad to hear you speak so, Lady Charity," she said, as the quiet knock to the door came again, announcing the arrival of their afternoon callers. "Now, let us be pleasant but firm. Steadfast and determined."

Charity nodded and rose to her feet.

"Of course, Lady Hayward," she answered, just before her chaperone called for them to enter.

"You must be wondering why we have called, Lady Hayward."

Charity reached out and lifted her teacup and saucer, glancing towards Lady Hayward as she did so. Both Lady Dewsbury and Lady Norwich had been present for some ten minutes and with the tea already poured, it now appeared time for them both to speak purposefully about what their true reasons were for coming to Lady Hayward's home.

"You are welcome to call, Lady Dewsbury, without

any particular reason," Lady Hayward answered, speaking quite calmly and with a small, if not rather cool smile on her face. "There is no need to express any reason, as such."

"Oh, but we must!" Lady Norwich exclaimed, as Charity took a sip of her tea and did her best to remain quite calm. "There has clearly been some sort of misunderstanding and we did not want either yourself or Lady Charity to be left in a state of confusion!"

Lady Hayward blinked in surprise, then looked towards Charity, her eyebrows lifting.

"Confusion?" she repeated, as Charity allowed herself a small smile. "Forgive me, Lady Norwich, but I assure you that there is no confusion here at present."

"Oh?" Lady Norwich's eagerness seemed to leave her as she looked towards her mother – and Charity did not miss the way that Lady Dewsbury frowned at her daughter, clearly encouraging her not to stray from their predetermined path. "That is to say, I am glad that there is no confusion. I should not like Lord Hosmer's intentions to have been so misconstrued."

Charity bit her lip and forced herself not to speak harshly, not to retort to the lady. Instead, she took in a breath and waited for a moment or two before she responded.

"There is no confusion when it comes to Lord Hosmer," she said, quite firmly. "I can assure you of that, Lady Norwich." Lady Norwich's eyes glittered with a malevolence that threatened to steal some of Charity's confidence but, with an effort, she continued to speak in the same calm, quiet tone as she had done before. "Lord

Hosmer has made himself very clear when it comes to our acquaintance," she continued, as Lady Norwich sighed plaintively and shook her head. "I have no doubts or fears in that regard, Lady Norwich, I can assure you of that."

"I am afraid that you are quite mistaken there, Lady Charity," came the swift reply. "Last evening, once you had departed, Lord Hosmer sought me out."

"He did," Lady Dewsbury interrupted, as though her word would give all the more assurance to Charity's heart. "He did find my daughter and spoke to her at length."

No flare of doubt stole Charity's breath and she remained precisely as she was, with what she hoped was a disbelieving expression on her face.

"I see," she replied, in a somewhat bored tone, before reaching for her tea again.

"He has told me that I was quite right to come to him as I did," Lady Norwich continued, her voice growing a little more fervent. "That he had been torn between myself and you, Lady Charity. I do not begrudge him that, for I have caused him great pain. And yet, despite that, he has decided to –"

"I will interrupt you, Lady Norwich, before you can speak further untruths." Charity shifted slightly in her chair, looking at the young lady with a steady gaze and seeing the color begin to drain from Lady Norwich's cheeks. "I do not and *will* not accept any words from you in this regard. There is nothing that you can say that I will believe. Lord Hosmer has done all he can to separate himself from you and from the past grievances and hurts that he has endured. Everything that he has said to me, I believe. I trust him and his words. Therefore, I must confess that whatever it is *you* say, I cannot help but ignore. I will not believe it, Lady Norwich, for your words mean nothing to me."

Silence filled the room for some minutes after Charity had finished speaking. Lady Hayward's expression was one of pride – she was clearly delighted with all that Charity had said and willing to stand directly by her side, should it be required of her. The words themselves, Charity realized, were all quite true. She *did* trust Lord Hosmer. To have allowed such doubts into her mind had been quite foolish, for it was now clear that Lady Norwich was, for whatever reason, attempting to manipulate her into stepping away from Lord Hosmer, in order that she herself might then move into Charity's place. Charity was not about to allow her to do so.

"I think you should show Lady Charity the letter which was sent to you, only this morning," Lady Dewsbury said quietly, as Lady Norwich suddenly began to nod, her fingers feverishly raking around her reticule as she looked for the item in question. "That, perhaps, will make her believe what you say."

Charity frowned and glanced towards Lady Hayward, who gave a small shake of her head. It was a clear indication that she ought not to believe this either, but a letter, however, was a good deal more important than mere hearsay. Lady Norwich finally pulled out a folded piece of paper and, with a look of triumph, handed it to Charity, who chose, instead, to simply place it on the table between herself and Lady Norwich rather than opening it to read.

"Whatever are you doing, Lady Charity?" Lady Dewsbury exclaimed, as Charity turned her gaze towards the lady. "This is proof that what my daughter says is quite true."

"I shall not accept it either," Charity replied, steadily. "I do not know whether or not Lord Hosmer has written this to you, Lady Norwich, save for your word."

"*And,*" Lady Norwich interrupted, a gleam in her eye, "by his signature and his seal, which you will find both of kept within the letter."

For a moment, a stab of doubt pushed its way into Charity's heart, but she tossed it aside with an effort.

"I do not wish to read it."

"Then I shall!" Lady Dewsbury rose from her chair in a flurry of skirts, making her way across towards Charity and snatching up the letter. Charity was so caught up in this that she did not notice the butler enter and speak quietly to Lady Hayward. Nor did she see the lady nod and reply to the butler, who then left the room on hasty feet. Rather, she watched as Lady Dewsbury shook out the letter and, as though she were about to make a great speech, cleared her throat gently, looked meaningfully towards Charity and then began.

"This letter reads, '*My dearest lady, I cannot help but allow my thoughts to return to you. Many times they have done so and I now permit them to consider you whenever they wish. I have struggled with our parting, have found myself lost without your presence and your company. Tell me that you will return to me soon so that I might no longer feel such great torment within my heart!'"* Lady Dewsbury turned the paper around and, with a confident smile on her face, thrust it in Charity's direction. "And there, Lady Charity, you will see his signature *and* his seal."

Charity looked unwillingly at the letter, seeing the signature of Lord Hosmer as well as the small wax seal that had been pressed beside it, as though to assure the reader that it *was* from him and could not be mistaken as to be from any other. Her mind began to whirl with questions, her brow furrowing as she looked back into Lady Dewsbury's face and saw the triumphant confidence there.

Had she been mistaken?

"That letter may very well have been from me, Lady Dewsbury, but was not written last evening, nor last week, nor last month," came a firm voice from behind Lady Dewsbury. "In fact, I believe I wrote that to Lady Norwich some years ago."

Charity's hands gripped the sides of her chair and she made to rise, only to sink back down into her seat as Lord Hosmer strode towards Lady Dewsbury and plucked the letter from her hand. Clearly somewhere between astonishment and horror, Lady Dewsbury's color became somewhat ashen and she dropped back into her chair without a sound, allowing Lord Hosmer to make his way towards Charity, looking down at her with a firm yet tender gaze.

"This letter was written when I was courting Lady Norwich," he told her, handing her the note. "I have written the date at the top of the page, although the year, it seems, has been inexplicably smudged."

Her heart beating furiously, Charity took the letter from him and saw that what he had said was quite true. Her hands trembled as she looked back at Lady Norwich, seeing the lady's face also now deathly pale, her plans and schemes entirely interrupted.

"You came to convince Lady Charity that there was something of great importance between us, Lady Norwich," Lord Hosmer said, turning to face the lady as Charity folded up the old letter again. "Lady Charity, I can only beg your forgiveness at my tardiness. I thought to come to you as soon as I could, to explain all, but the matter of discovering precisely *why* Lady Norwich and Lady Dewsbury had attempted to do such a thing was of great importance. I wanted to understand it so that I might explain." His lip curled and his jaw tightened as he held Lady Norwich's gaze, making Charity realize just how angry he was at what they had done. Her heart began to pound furiously as he placed his hands behind his back, his voice now more of a low growl than anything else. "You lack the financial security you once had, do you not?" he said, as Lady Norwich put one hand to her mouth. "Lord Norwich did not leave you with much in his will, and you were required to return to Lord and Lady Dewsbury. However, it seems that Lord Dewsbury has a few debts of his own, that he also struggles to maintain the financial standing that you were both quite used to enjoying a few years ago. Therefore, the only way that you might be able to relieve yourself of such a burden, Lady Norwich, was to find someone who might wed you. Someone who was of good standing. And the match had to be made in haste, for the matter was urgent and you could not afford to allow any other to discover the truth of your situation." He glanced back towards Charity, who felt a great swell of relief flow through her soul. "Therefore, you chose me, despite the fact that I have secured my interest in another." Charity smiled at him a little tentatively, aware now that Lady Dewsbury and Lady Norwich had attempted to manipulate both herself and Lord Hosmer for their own ends. Lord Hosmer's expression softened for just a moment as he held her gaze, before he turned back to speak to the other ladies. "You had made discreet enquiries and discovered that, not only did I return to London every Christmas season, I also remained in dull spirits and seemed to find no enjoyment in anything at all. Therefore, you hoped that I would be easily encouraged back into your arms, back into your embrace – whereas, Lady Norwich, the precise opposite is true."

"Please!" Lady Dewsbury exclaimed, swiping the air with her hand. "That is more than enough, Lord Hosmer! You have said all that is needed."

Lord Hosmer shook his head.

"I thought I had done so, Lady Dewsbury," he answered, gravely, "but it seems that both you and your daughter are unable to either hear what I say or accept it as the truth. You have tried to set myself and Lady Charity asunder, in the vain hope that I will return to the lady I once believed I cared for. I can assure you both, for what is the final time, that I will never again return to your company or to your affections, Lady Norwich." His shoulders lifted slightly and Charity felt the strength of his words fill the room, her heart swelling with the determination that was expressed within them.

"I have come to realize my foolishness in losing the happiness and the joy that could have been mine these last years, if only I had been willing to set the past aside and look instead to the future. But, at the same time, I am glad that I did not for, had I done so, then I might never have encountered Lady Charity, I might never have discovered the depths of affection that can be in one's heart. I could never have found the true satisfaction and contentment with knowing that deep sense of trust which can form between two persons. And therefore, Lady Norwich, nothing you can say or do will ever tempt me to neglect the happiness which I have found here. You must find another man willing to step into your scheme."

Nothing was said for some minutes after Lord Hosmer had finished. Charity discovered that she was breathing very hard indeed, looking from Lady Dewsbury to Lady Norwich and back again, seeing equal expressions of shock mingled with dismay written on both their faces. Evidently, they had both been quite certain that Lord Hosmer would return to Lady Norwich's arms without hesitation, and the fact that he had not done so had ruined their plans entirely.

"I think," Lady Hayward said briskly, as she rose from her chair, "that the matter here is concluded. Lady Norwich, Lady Dewsbury, allow me to show you to the door."

She did not wait for them to agree nor even to rise from their chairs but walked promptly to the door and stood there, patiently waiting. Charity too rose from her chair and made her way to stand by Lord Hosmer, who looked down at her with a gentleness in his eyes that restored every last piece of her heart.

"Your refusal leaves us with almost nothing," Lady Dewsbury said, her voice shrill and cutting through the room with a great fierceness that stole Charity's attention away from Lord Hosmer. "If you would only agree, then Lady Norwich would be restored! Your selfishness is utterly breathtaking, Lord Hosmer."

He inclined his head in a half bow.

"Good afternoon, Lady Dewsbury," he replied, clearly no longer willing to argue with the lady. "I do not think that any selfishness in this matter is mine, Lady Dewsbury, nor do I think that we will often be in each other's company again."

Lady Dewsbury's face flushed a deep crimson and, for a few moments, it appeared as though she were about to say something in retaliation, only for her to turn her head away and flounce towards the door. Lady Norwich, Charity noticed, had dropped her head in evident shame and when she lifted it for only a moment to glance up at them both, Charity saw tears on the lady's cheeks. A stab of compassion ran through her, realizing that the lady was truly in difficulty although, of course, she had attempted to resolve the situation in a most improper and incorrect fashion.

"Good afternoon, Lady Norwich," she said, gently. "I do hope that you will find a resolution to your difficulties soon."

She spoke genuinely but the lady did not answer her,

shaking her head and turning away from them both with hurried steps. In only a few minutes, Charity found herself entirely alone with Lord Hosmer and, looking up at him saw the same relief etched into his features as she felt within her heart.

"My dear Lady Charity," he murmured, turning towards her so that he might take both of her hands in his. "Forgive me for last evening. I should have spoken with more decisiveness, with greater firmness!"

She shook her head.

"It was not a situation of your making, Lord Hosmer," she told him, softly. "I do not blame you for what occurred, truly."

"Then you are most generous," he replied, lifting her hand to his lips for a moment. Charity's cheeks warmed as heat rushed up her arm towards her heart, her smile dazzling. "But I know already of your great kindness of spirit, your generosity of heart and your sweet nature, Lady Charity. When I feared that I had broken things between us, when I grew afraid that you might turn from me, my heart was aching with such a great and desperate pain that I could barely sleep! This morning, I awoke with a resolve to sort the matter out entirely – and thus, I have done so."

"You have," she answered him, letting go of his hand for a moment so that she might reach up and press her palm to his cheek, seeing the tenderness in his eyes and finding herself quite overwhelmed by it. "But you would not have lost me, Lord Hosmer. I confess I was a little confused, a little doubtful, but realizing now what Lady

Norwich was attempting to do, I have full understanding."

Lord Hosmer closed his eyes and pressed his hand to hers.

"There is so much more that I wish to say to you, Lady Charity," he told her, his eyes opening and meeting her own. "I – I should like you to know that everything I said to Lady Norwich about what I have learned from you and what I now feel for you is nothing but the truth." Taking her hand in his, he settled it over his heart and bent his head just a little, his words quiet and yet spoken with such force that Charity could barely catch her breath. "My heart is filled with none but you, Lady Charity. I should like to speak to your father about my intentions, but before I do, I must know if I am to have any hope."

Charity looked up into his eyes and felt her heart singing with joy.

"Can you not hear the song of my heart, Lord Hosmer?" she asked, gently. "Can you not hear it sing with the joy of knowing that the affection it has within it is returned?"

His eyes flared and he put one hand to her waist, pulling her a little closer.

"Then you will accept my courtship?" he asked, a little hoarsely. "You will be glad of a closer acquaintance with me?"

Charity smiled back at him, her whole being flooded with joy.

"Very glad indeed, Lord Hosmer," she answered, quietly, "for, in truth, it is all that I want."

EPILOGUE

B enedict could not recall when he had enjoyed a happier Christmas. The ivy and holly that decorated each and every room they entered filled his heart with an almost inexplicable joy, and the company had been most excellent indeed. Much to his surprise – as well as to the surprise of Lady Charity – the Duke of Landon and his younger daughters had all arrived in London in time for Christmas Day. Lord and Lady Ramsbury had invited the Duke and his daughters to join the rest of them for Christmas Day and, thus far, Benedict had enjoyed every moment.

Apparently, the Duke had been thinking of coming to London for Christmas Day for some time but had not informed Lady Charity of it, in case he had changed his mind. However, Benedict was very glad that the gentleman had chosen to come, for it gave him the opportunity not only to greet the man, but also to speak to him openly about his intentions towards Lady Charity. He and the Duke had already spoken at length earlier that day, prior to their attendance at church and, much to Benedict's relief, the Duke had appeared quite at ease over the match.

He sighed contentedly to himself as he sat back, his plate of plum pudding now quite empty. Across the table, he smiled at Lady Charity, who blushed but smiled back at him.

"Gentlemen, the port?" Ramsbury cried, as the ladies rose from the table. "Or shall we take it with us to the drawing room?"

"To the drawing room, surely!" Lady Ramsbury cried, as Ramsbury laughed. "We must sing together! I am sure that one of the ladies present will be able to play a good many Christmas songs for us to enjoy!"

"And the yule log is in the fire too," Ramsbury agreed, pushing himself out of his chair with an effort. "Very well, my dear, you have convinced me. Shall we make our way to the drawing room, Your Grace?"

Benedict rose from his chair and made his way to the door, lingering behind some of the others so that he might be last to make his way from the room. His eyes met Lady Charity's and, as Lady Hayward stepped from the room, he reached out and caught Lady Charity's hand, pulling her close to him rather than permitting her to go through the door.

"I have spoken to your father."

Lady Charity smiled up at him, clearly quite willing to remain with him for a few moments.

"I have heard," she replied, her hazel eyes softening as she held his gaze. "My father has been very open with me about his consideration of you."

Benedict frowned.

"Oh?"

"He thinks you *most* suitable," she answered, laughing quietly. "You did not expect anything else, surely?"

Relief tore through him.

"Then – then you will accept my courtship?" he asked, as Lady Charity nodded. "You must know, surely, that my intention is matrimony, Lady Charity. I will be honest with you in that."

Her smile spread all the wider and, much to his astonishment, she wrapped her arms about his neck, closing the distance between them. His hands settled on her waist, his breath hitching at her nearness.

"My intentions are much the same, Lord Hosmer," she told him, teasingly. "I am only glad that my father has been so quick to agree."

"As am I," he replied, looking down into her face and seeing such a beauty there that he could not take his gaze from her. "Charity, my heart holds a great love for you. A love that I do not believe will ever fade. Each Christmas, I shall remember all that you have done, all that you have given me, and I shall find afresh that happiness which fills me at this very moment."

Lady Charity let out a long, contented sigh.

"I too have found a greater happiness than I could ever have imagined," she told him, her gaze still holding fast to his. "I love you also, Lord Hosmer... Benedict, if I may call you so? I believe I always shall."

Benedict glanced up and then shook his head, letting out a heavy sigh as he did so.

"If only there were a kissing bough above our heads, Charity," he murmured. "Then I might be inclined towards kissing you."

She laughed up at him, her hands tightening just a fraction.

"But it is Christmas Day, Benedict," she answered, as his head began to lower. "And I believe that on days such as this, you are permitted to steal a kiss, should the lady be willing?"

A smile tugged at the corner of his mouth.

"And are you willing, Charity?" he asked, as he continued to slowly lower his head.

"I am," she whispered, before finally meeting his lips with her own.

I HOPE you enjoyed Lady Charity and Lord Hosmer's story!He now has some precious memories of the Christmas season to replace the terrible ones!

Here's another Christmas story just for you! Love and Christmas Wishes: Three Regency Romance Novellas

Check out the first couple chapters just ahead!

A SNEAK PEEK OF LOVE AND CHRISTMAS WISHES

"What if I see him again? What shall I do?" Sarah Powell groaned as she hid her face in her hands.

"Sarah, you must steel yourself for the unpleasant truth that you must face Mr. Grainger again. It cannot be helped. If you are to accompany us to his father's house of Hatherley Hall, then you will see him. What other choice do you have? Are you to remain here at the vicarage, alone, as the staff goes about their duties?" replied a young woman with a slightly dismissive air. "This matter was settled in the summer. Why are you worrying about it now?"

"Jane, can you not see that our dear cousin is mortified?" said a second woman as she rushed to Sarah's side. With her characteristic grace, Katie Brookes sat on the bed beside Sarah, wrapping her arm around her shoulders.

Sarah peered at her oldest cousin, Jane Brookes, the eldest of two sisters. Jane was standing in front of her in the middle of a modest bedroom that was opulently furnished in shades of ivory and green, whilst her younger sister, Katie, was sitting beside Sarah on the bed. The bedclothes, the chairs, and the curtains were embroidered in the same ivy and flower patterns that matched the shade of green damask covering the walls. The effect was somewhat like a garden, which only added to Sarah's discomfort as she recalled the summertime.

With crossed arms, Jane Brookes appeared stern. Her plain and unremarkable face was set in a frown as she looked at her sister Katie and her cousin, Sarah.

"Sarah, I understand that you are embarrassed. I am not trying to be unfeeling, but this is hardly the time to make your complaints known. We are leaving for our Christmas visit to Hatherley in an hour. Our trunks have been packed and loaded, and the carriages will be brought around to the front of the house at any moment."

"Maybe I should remain here at the vicarage where I will be no trouble to anyone," Sarah sighed.

Katie, the beauty of the sisters, looked at her cousin Sarah with big blue eyes filled with kindness as she said, "Please, do not worry, Sarah. How dreadful to think of you all alone here when we are away at the ball. It would be terrible, and I would not enjoy myself in the least. You must come with us, you must! I know that Hatherley Hall is only a few miles away, but we are residing with the family for a few days, and I simply cannot be without you. Say that you will attend?"

"I want to go, I do. Believe me, I do not want to be here all by myself. After what happened between Mr. Grainger and I, I cannot bear to see him again. How foolish I was to think he wanted to marry me," Sarah said quietly, "How can I face him when I have been so ridiculous?"

With her hands on her hips, Jane let out a heavy sigh, "That incident was not your fault. I have spoken with Mr. Grainger about it. He agrees that he never intended for your acquaintance to become romantic. He has apologized for his lapse of judgment."

"Jane, I cannot disagree with you regarding his conduct. He has apologized. I have forgiven him, but it does not change how badly I misjudged his feelings. How will I ever find the courage to look him in the eye?"

"You will face him, and you will see that you and he can, at the very least, become friends. It was all a terrible blunder. I know those words do not lessen the hardship you may feel, but you must confess that he has behaved as a gentleman," Jane explained.

"So he has, I cannot fault him for his behavior in the slightest. I wish he had told me that he had no interest in marrying me at the start. I know I seem to be very silly indeed, but I truly thought he held me in the same high regard as I held him."

Jane sat on the other side of Sarah, "Do not think of my statements as being evidence that I am uncaring towards your feelings, I am not. Mr. Grainger is one of my dearest friends. I have known him and his sister for many years. I do not believe he ever meant to embarrass you. When you see him again, when he treats you as amicably as he does me or Katie, you will soon discover that he does not think less of you."

"Did I misunderstand him?" Sarah asked Jane.

"No," Jane answered, "You did not misunderstand

him. It is not your fault that his father is the Baron Carmody."

"Sarah, be cheerful. You may not have any money of your own, but you are accomplished," Katie suggested in her melodic bright voice. "Your countenance is pleasing as any woman in Cheltham. Mr. Grainger may have slipped out of your grasp, but you will find a gentleman who may not mind that you only possess a modest dowry."

"Is that supposed to cheer her?" Jane asked as she patted Sarah on the hand.

"Yes, it is. Besides, I will let you borrow my second favorite gown for the ball. With your light hair and your eyes such a striking shade of green, you will look so delightful that Mr. Grainger will regret not asking you to marry him!"

Katie's attempts at kindness stung Sarah even though she knew her cousin did not mean to inflict any insult or offense. It was true that she did not have the money for any new gowns or even a pair of new kid gloves. Looking down at her plain cream-colored afternoon dress reminded her of her status as a companion to her two wealthy cousins, although Katie was the one who was always given more than her sister. In their beautiful, colorful gowns, they appeared as exotic as tropical birds compared to Sarah. Jane was wearing a long sleeve carriage dress in a crimson hue, while her sister Katie, the acknowledged pale beauty, was wearing an exquisite frock of light blue. Of course, Katie's gown was a good deal finer than her sister's, given that their mother favored one daughter over the other.

"Thank you, Katie," Sarah replied as she took a deep breath, "I do appreciate your kindness, both of you. I am sorry to be so much trouble. I cannot think what came over me. I have not thought of Mr. Grainger very much these past few months but when the prospect of seeing him again came near, I was overwhelmed by embarrassment."

"Think nothing of it. I am certain that what you feel is due entirely to lack of rest. You have been occupied by the preparations for the holiday, have you not?" Jane said with a smile, obviously trying to put the thought of Mr. Grainger from Sarah's mind

Sarah nodded, "I have been preoccupied as of late. Katie's new gowns had to be fitted and ready to be packed. Then there was the matter of the new pelisses, spencers and matching afternoon dresses."

Katie nodded, although Sarah noticed that she looked rather awkward over the fact that her sister had not been given as many new gowns as she. "You are not as anxious about Mr. Grainger as you thought," Katie said, turning her attention back to Sarah. "Smile and forget that you were ever concerned about seeing him again. I shall not remember it, and neither shall Jane," she suggested.

"Perhaps you are right, Katie," Sarah offered, although she did not believe it. She knew very well that she wished she would never see him again, not after she made the mistake of presuming he felt more for her than he declared. If she could only return to the summer when she last visited Hatherley Hall, she would never act so ridiculously.

"You are simply fatigued from the added responsibilities mother has heaped upon your shoulders. It really seems unfair when we have the maid to see to our wardrobes. Why mother demands that you oversee the ordering of new clothes for the holiday is a mystery and wholly unnecessary," clucked Jane.

"I do not mind. Your family has been generous to take me in and give me a position. If I must do an additional task to earn my keep, I am prepared to do all that your mother would ask of me," Sarah replied, as she tried to smile.

A sudden rapping at the door announced the entrance of Mrs. Brookes, Jane and Katie's mother. She was as unremarkable in her appearance as Jane, but her face had thinned over the years. Lines crept around her eyes and her mouth, leaving her expression practically a permanent frown, most likely the result of scowling at servants and her family. As she bustled into the room, she turned her attention to Sarah, her expression as dour as ever as she demanded, "Sarah, are the trunks packed and loaded? Have you made every effort to ensure that we have included all of the gloves we will need? What of the jewelry?"

Sarah was quick to jump to her feet. In her despair, she had forgotten her duties as a companion. As she thought of an answer, her cousin Jane replied in her stead, "Mother, we have everything we require, packed and on the carriages. It is not as though we are going for a prolonged stay! There is no need to question Sarah about it, it is already done."

Mrs. Brookes glared at her eldest daughter, "I will bother her as much I choose, who are you to answer for her after all I have done for her? Sarah, why are you here in Katie's room? If the trunks are loaded, you should be downstairs seeing that the cook and the maid understand their duties while we are away."

Sarah bristled at her Aunt's reminder that it was her generosity which sustained her and kept her living under the roof of the Brookes house in Cheltham. Despite the urge to reply that she would do well without anyone's charity, she recalled that she did rely on their kindness. Resigned to her status as poor cousin and companion, she answered, "Yes, Aunt, I will see to it this instant."

"I hope so, slovenly behavior will not be accepted. I doubt that this laziness was addressed at your last position," Mrs. Brookes remarked.

As Sarah left the bedroom, she overheard her cousin Jane defend her as Mrs. Brookes dismissed her objections to fawn over her youngest daughter. The door closed behind her. She was alone in the hallway of the vicarage, as she was alone in life. She was a woman who had no prospects other than to be a companion or a governess. With her head hung low, she made her way down the narrow corridor of the vicarage, descending the stairs to the kitchen.

Aside from the usual amount of jostling and shimmying along the snowy roads leading from Cheltham out into the countryside, the carriage ride from the vicarage to Hatherley was pleasant. The interior of the carriage was reasonably warm despite the cold of mid-December. In her hand-me-down pelisse lined with fur, her gloved hands in the matching second-hand fur muff, Sarah found the journey not altogether uncomfortable. She rode in the second carriage with Jane and the maid that would attend her cousins, as Katie rode with her parents at her mother's insistence in the first carriage. There was no question in Sarah's mind that Katie was her mother's favorite of all three of her children, an observation that she did not share with Jane whom, she was sure, was all too aware of it.

"I hope Henry arrives tonight. He said he was coming to Hatherley." Jane murmured, half to herself, as she spoke of her brother, the eldest of the Brookes children and the only son.

"That would be wonderful. How are his classes? Is he doing well?"

"He has not written otherwise, so I can presume that he is first in his studies and examinations. If he was having trouble, I have no doubt he would have written to tell me about it."

"What will he do after he finishes university? Does he still wish to enter the clergy?" Sarah asked, even though she knew that was the plan for her cousin, Henry Brookes.

"Will father give him any other choice?" Jane asked, with a tired air, "He is the son of a vicar, He will follow suit, as is expected, else I shall be greatly astonished."

"As will I. He seems suited for the role as vicar. He has your father's compassion and charm."

"I have often thought that as well. If only our Mother was not disappointed in his interest in pursuing an honorable profession. She was hoping he would become a solicitor or find an heiress to marry for her money."

Sarah did not say anything in response to Jane's comments about her mother. How well Sarah recalled her aunt's invitation for her to come live at the vicarage as a companion. It was the single gesture of sisterly affection Mrs. Brookes showed Sarah's mother and one that she never permitted Sarah to forget. Sarah pushed that unpleasant thought away as she replied, "Henry knows his own mind. If he wants to join the church, he will not be dissuaded."

"Perhaps he can find a position of curate after he finishes his studies. One day, Mr. Putnam might well work for my brother, as he does now for my father. How strange that would be!" Sarah thought of Mr. Putnam, the gentleman who was the vicar's steward, having taken the place of his late father. He was a quiet studious man, steadfast and reliable. She wondered what he would do if the time came to seek another position, an uncertainty that she understood all too well.

"Do you think he will want to work with someone other than your father? I always imagined Henry would take your father's place in Cheltham when your father retired."

"It is my father's desire that he do so, but I have a feeling my brother has an adventurous side of him. He has often told me that he wishes to journey to the Indies, to pursue work as a missionary, but I doubt he will ever go as far as London."

"And he is to be at Hatherley Hall this evening?"

"Yes," Jane agreed. "He is residing there as a guest already, given that he is such good friends with George. But now, I think, we shall talk of another subject, one that I hesitate to mention," Jane said as she peered at Sarah.

Sarah slipped her hands out of the fur muff in an effort to distract herself as she felt the unwavering gaze of her cousin. Jane was not often direct in her speech, choosing to keep her thoughts to herself more often than not. However, on the occasion that Jane chose to speak, Sarah knew that she had thought long and hard about saying whatever it was that was on her mind. Sarah admired her cousin but did not have the luxury of Jane's dowry or her place in society to speak as she wished.

Seeing Jane's small smile, Sarah could no longer withstand her cousin's penetrating stare as she asked, "What is it? What do you wish to say? Is it about my silly behavior regarding Mr. Grainger? I apologize. I have never been so ashamed in all of my life."

Jane's voice was gentle. "You are courageous to return to Hatherley to face him again, I should not be able to if it were me. No, my dear cousin, that is not the subject I wish to discuss. I wish to offer you an apology."

Sarah was dumbfounded, "What reason could you have for offering me an apology?"

"I am not proud of Mother's actions earlier. She is my mother and of course, I respect her, but I do not know why she insists on treating you so condescendingly at every turn. You have done nothing to deserve her treatment of you."

Sarah was relieved that the subject of Mr. Grainger had been supplanted by a subject which vexed her but did not cause her to feel like she would like to run away. She saw that Jane meant what she said, that she was genuinely moved by affection to offer an apology for her own mother's behavior. Sarah decided to answer as delicately as possible.

"Jane, it is good of you to apologize on behalf of your mother, but it is unnecessary. Your mother has every reason to remind me of my place in your household. It is by her generosity that I have a home to live in and a salary."

"You are too good, dear Sarah. It vexes me in the utmost to see my mother treat you as if you were a person of no consequence."

"I *am* a person of no consequence," Sarah stated.

"I do not believe it. Just because your mother married

for love and was driven from her parents' house does not make my mother's treatment of you any less disgraceful."

"It is a burden I have borne for my entire life. I have learned to live with it.," Sarah shrugged as she tried to remain calm. If she told the truth, she truly found it a most difficult burden.

She struggled more than she dared say aloud. The circumstances of her birth were not as unfortunate as Mrs. Brookes may have judged them to be. Her mother married a lieutenant with barely enough money to pay for his commission. When he died of fever, he left an insignificant income for Sarah and her mother. Yet, Sarah knew that was not her fault, and neither was it regrettable. It was people like her aunt who reminded her that she was lowly, that she was a woman who was barely more than a servant. When she was alone in the small cottage she shared with her mother, she did not wish for riches or luxuries. It was when she was in the presence of lords and ladies, of wealthy daughters and eligible gentlemen, that she was reminded of her inferior birth.

"I do mind," Jane stated, firmly. "I mind how you are treated. If I am rude to you in any way, know that I do not mean to be. It has nothing to do with your modest upbringing, but everything to do with my own inability to act in accordance with the slightest of decorum."

Thinking that Jane was making herself out to be a good deal worse than she truly was, Sarah shook her head. Jane was always polite and somewhat reserved, and the fact that she wanted to apologize for her mother's lack of respect towards Sarah spoke of her sweetness of character. "I admire your kind heart, Jane. I wish I had the freedom to be more like you in that respect," Sarah confessed.

"No, you do not. You have no need to. You are the epitome of a lady even if you do not carry the title. With your natural grace and charm, I shall be very surprised if you do not convince a duke to wed you. If you do, where will my mother be? She will have to sit below you at dinner and address you as my lady? What a lark that would be! I pray it happens simply to see the look of astonishment on her face."

Sarah laughed at her cousin's suggestions. Jane had a way of always cheering her, of making her feel better.

"That would be humorous, the idea that I will become a duchess. It's far more possible that I should become the next queen before that happened."

Jane giggled, "You never can tell, for, after all, it is Christmas and magic is afoot."

Sarah rolled her eyes, mischievously, knowing that Christmas day itself was still over a month away. "If only there was a way to magically mend my pride in that time, so the sight of Mr. Grainger does not affect me in the slightest," she said as she gazed out of the carriage window.

"Do not be concerned with Mr. Grainger. I am certain that you will find that he will make every effort to offer amends when we arrive at his family's home."

"Which, unless I am greatly mistaken, is in the distance," observed Sarah as she peered out the window at the vast landscape of the Cotswolds.

In winter, the bucolic country setting of the Cotswolds was a serene reflection of the season in all its glory. Snow covered the tops of the gently rolling hill-sides. Ice sparkled in the late afternoon light as it encased the dark branches of the trees which lined the roadway. Snow fell gently outside the carriage framing the view of the stately Tudor mansion in the valley below.

Hatherley Hall was the name of the house. The grand residence was commonly referred to as Hatherley by the local gentry, the villagers of Cheltham, and the nearby market town of Abbeford Hills. The hall, or house as it was referred to, was a tall structure built of brick with high pointed roofs and gables. The windows were narrow stained glass at the front entrance giving the house a gothic air. With its forest of chimneys reaching into the sky and the tree-lined avenue, leading to the house itself, the effect was impressive and imposing. Sarah imagined that the first Baron Carmody who commissioned the house must have demanded that it be an imposing residence. As much as she dreaded seeing Mr. Grainger again, she looked forward to a few days of holiday revels inside this historic mansion.

"I am pleased we have arrived before sundown. I hope we are not late for dinner. I am famished!" Jane exclaimed.

Sarah did not know if she would be able to eat a bite the entire time she was a guest at Hatherley. Her own humiliation was too much to bear but bear it she must for the sake of her cousins. As Jane reminded her, she and Katie had known the heir to the title and his younger brother all of their lives. The Graingers were a good sort to be aristocrats regardless of the events of the previous summer. Sarah decided she would endeavor to forgive

Mr. Grainger even if he had led her to believe he harbored feelings for her.

"I hope we will be given the rooms in the west wing. How I adore the tower, it makes me feel like an archer of old as I prepare to defend the castle," Jane exclaimed.

"What an imagination you have! If I were to find myself in the tower room, I would think of myself as a princess," Sarah stated.

With a confident manner, Jane held her head high as she remarked, "Then you shall be a princess and I will be an archer. Together we shall do what must to be cheerful until Twelfth Night."

"I hope we have a good few days here, but I do not know how joyous it will be for me. I will be the only woman in attendance who could be mistaken for a maid."

"Sarah, you can wear any of my dresses if you choose. I promise that you shall have a wonderful time. Do not torment yourself about your present circumstances. Not when there is celebrating and merriment to be had. We can return to our gloomy lives, you and I, when we arrive home again in a few days."

Reaching for her muff, Sarah slid her hands inside the cozy warmth of it, as she leaned back into the velvet seat of the carriage. She promised herself she would not be gloomy, no matter how much she wished to be. Jane was correct. It was the month of Christmas, she was a guest of the Baron Carmody. She would enjoy cards, music, a ball, and delicious food for a time before returning to her own modest life at the vicarage. She would be a fool not to endeavor to have a splendid time. With her mind on the upcoming schedule of diverting recreation, she tried to quell her nervousness. She was going to Hatherley, just as she had during the summer. She hoped that this time, she would come home with delightful memories.

SARAH WILL HAVE to face Mr. Grainger soon. Hope it is not too painful! Perhaps she might meet someone else during her stay? Check it the rest of the story on the Kindle Store. Love and Christmas Wishes: Three Regency Romance Novellas

MY DEAR READER

Thank you for reading and supporting my books! I hope this story brought you some escape from the real world into the always captivating Regency world. A good story, especially one with a happy ending, just brightens your day and makes you feel good! If you enjoyed the book, would you leave a review on Amazon? Reviews are always appreciated.

Below is a complete list of all my books! Why not click and see if one of them can keep you entertained for a few hours?

The Duke's Daughters Series
The Duke's Daughters: A Sweet Regency Romance
Boxset
A Rogue for a Lady
My Restless Earl
Rescued by an Earl
In the Arms of an Earl
The Reluctant Marquess (Prequel)

A Smithfield Market Regency Romance
The Smithfield Market Romances: A Sweet Regency
Romance Boxset
The Rogue's Flower

Saved by the Scoundrel
Mending the Duke
The Baron's Malady

The Returned Lords of Grosvenor Square
The Returned Lords of Grosvenor Square: A Regency
Romance Boxset
The Waiting Bride
The Long Return
The Duke's Saving Grace
A New Home for the Duke

The Spinsters Guild
A New Beginning
The Disgraced Bride
A Gentleman's Revenge
A Foolish Wager
A Lord Undone

Convenient Arrangements
A Broken Betrothal
In Search of Love
Wed in Disgrace
Betrayal and Lies
A Past to Forget
Engaged to a Friend

Landon House
Mistaken for a Rake
A Selfish Heart
A Love Unbroken

A Christmas Match

Happy Reading!
All my love,
Rose

Made in the USA
Middletown, DE
08 April 2021